Mining
the
Iron
Mask

GEORGE CORY FRANKLIN

Mining
the
Iron
Mask

ILLUSTRATED BY
WILLIAM MOYERS

ARIEL BOOKS ～ NEW YORK

ARIEL BOOKS

A DIVISION OF
PELLEGRINI & CUDAHY

Chapter 1

THE SPRING TERM of high school in Del Norte, Colorado, had ended, so most of the students had left for their homes. Frank Mathews came into the deserted gym looking for his friend Roy Barnett. The expression on Frank's face was like that of a key football player who has had a kick blocked. He slammed the gym door shut behind him in disgust and threw himself onto a bench. His actions were wholly unlike his usual calm resourceful self to Roy, who at the moment was resting comfortably on the small of his back, his feet parked on the parallel bars.

Roy shook his head. "Gosh, Frank, what a lousy disposition for a fine spring morning. Why the gripe?"

"All right, I'm sore, so what? A lot you know about trouble. I could rave about sunshine, spring flowers and all that dribble if I had the chance of making money that you have."

Roy raised himself to a more dignified position. "You must be nuts if you think that a pack train of twenty burros is a fortune. What's ailing you?"

"Well, to be brief, that summer job I was counting on to pay my expenses in law school has fallen through. The man who promised me the job has just told me that he's not putting on any more help. Then I went to the law firm where I've been pounding out a few extra dollars by typing briefs. I got some more of the same. Judge Brewster advised me to forget the law profession. He says it's too crowded now." Frank leaned back against the wall in complete dejection. "Apparently the whole thing has been just a dream."

"I'm sorry," Roy apologized. "I suppose I should be grateful that I have even as much as I have. But it's no cinch to get enough money to start to college with the amount that a small train of burros will make."

Frank, surprised, forgot his own problem and asked, "Can't you get more burros? There seem to be plenty of them around here, and no one uses them any more now that trucks and railroads haul all the ore from the mines to the smelter."

"There are some mines that use them in the back country where they don't even have a telephone or portable radio as yet. The trails are blocked by snow for eight months of the year," Roy replied. "Just to show you, here is an advertisement I was reading when you came in. I cut it out of a Lake City paper."

Frank read aloud the clipping Roy handed him:

"WANTED. Pack train capable of transporting five tons of copper ore a day from the Legal Tender Mine at Carson, Colorado, to the end of the wagon road. Distance five miles. Rate, four dollars per ton. Will pay thirty cents a stick for lagging. Fifty cents for ten inch stulls to be packed from the Ironbed Park a distance of one and one-half miles. Write or apply to Charles Woodruff, Superintendent."

"That looks good," Frank said. "How much will a burro pack?"

"Two hundred pounds that distance—one trip a day."

"Then your train would handle less than half the amount this man wants packed."

"Right," Roy agreed.

"I'm no whiz at figures," Frank admitted. "But it would take fifty burros to handle that job. Could two men work that much stock, if they had them?"

"Sure. But I haven't got them, so I'm no more likely to go to Tech and become a mining engineer than you are to go to law school," Roy said.

"I still think that there ought to be some way of using some of the burros that are roaming all over the place," Frank said. "How much do saddles cost?"

"Twenty dollars each, with blankets and—"
Roy's face took on a tense expression. "Wait a
minute. Since your plans have gone bust, how
would you like to throw in with me as a partner?"

A wistful look came over Frank's face. "Could
I? I don't know a thing about packing."

"Well, you can learn, can't you?" Roy said.
"The man who runs the secondhand store down
near the depot bought a lot of burro saddles from
an outfit that went broke a couple of years ago.
There's no sale for them now. He might be willing to make a deal and give us a chance to pay
him a little each month."

"O.K. What are we waiting for?" Frank demanded. "Why not go talk to him? I know I'll be
awkward and green at first but I'll sure do my
best."

The secondhand store Roy had mentioned
was several blocks from the main center of Del
Norte, a village that had once been called "The
Gateway to the San Juan" at a time when the only
transportation had been horse-drawn vehicles
and pack outfits. The open space behind the
building was crowded with old rusty equipment,
freight wagons and stage coaches. Inside the

building, harnesses, saddles and all sorts of out-moded articles hung on the wall. These were marked at a very low price.

An old Scot arose from an antique desk. He greeted the boys cordially, hoping to sell them a fishing rod or possibly an old iron camp kettle. "Something this morning, boys?"

"We were thinking of a pack trip into the mountains," Roy began cautiously. "Have you any burro saddles?"

"Plenty of them." Mac Dermott led the way to a lean-to shed, where the burro saddles were stacked in a long row of neat piles.

Roy picked one up and shook the breeching and breast strap loose. They fell into natural positions, indicating that they had been well oiled and cared for before being put away. "How much?"

"How many do you want?" Mac Dermott asked, trying to keep the eagerness out of his eyes.

"We might be able to use several if the price is right," Roy answered.

"How about five dollars each?" Mac Dermott asked.

Roy, too, tried to keep from showing his feelings. "Does that include blankets?"

"Yes. And I have a bale of three-eighths-inch rope and one of one-half inch. I can fit them up complete for that price."

Roy looked at Frank. "Well, partner, what do you say?"

It was the first time Frank had felt the satisfaction of being consulted on business matters. He tried to meet the responsibility that the name Partner implied. "I think that's a fair price. But, suppose we think it over and come back later."

Mac Dermott knew the value of closing a deal immediately. "If it's a matter of money—" he began.

Roy was also anxious to close the deal. He decided there would be nothing gained by delay. He told Mac Dermott something of the plan they had worked out. When he mentioned thirty saddles, Mac Dermott grinned. One hundred and fifty dollars, even on credit, was more than he could expect to make for several weeks. In fact, he had about reached the conclusion that he would never sell that many of the saddles.

"If you're going to pack ore, you should have

a few extra saddles in case of one breaking. There are forty here. Pay me twenty-five dollars and give me your note, due in six months, for one hundred and fifty dollars and take the whole lot."

It was a tense moment for the boys. They both realized that the decision they made would commit them to a plan they had not fully worked out.

Mac Dermott saw that a slight push might put the sale over. "I'll throw in those two bales of rope," he added.

Frank took a billfold from his pocket. It contained four five-dollar bills. Roy took five silver dollars from his pocket. "I guess that settles it," he remarked as they handed the money to Mac Dermott.

Outside on the street the boys stopped to face the problem they had shouldered. Roy laid a hand on Frank's arm. "Was that twenty, by any chance, all you had?"

Frank's face flushed. "I had saved that to pay my next month's room rent. If we don't get out inside of a week, I'll be sleeping on the ground and digging roots to eat."

"We've sure got off to a risky start," Roy said. "We've got twenty burros, my two ponies and sixty saddles. We're not sure we can get the job. And we have no money with which to buy supplies. Fine thing!" He whistled.

"I've been thinking about that," Frank said. "I know where there are lots of burros. That advertisement says—'Apply in person or write.' How would it be for you to go to Carson and see this man Woodruff about the job? While you're gone, I'll find thirty burros and put them in that little pasture below town."

"That's a good idea as far as it goes," Roy replied. "But before we jump off the deep end again, let's be sure we can deliver what we agree to do. Let's go to the bank and see if we can borrow the necessary expense money."

Jim Campbell, the banker, had known Roy's father as a man of strict integrity. He listened sympathetically to Roy's request for a loan of two hundred dollars, asked several questions and did not reply at once. When he finally began to talk, the hopes of the boys sank to an all-time low.

"Your effort to make your own way does you great credit. If I personally could help you, I'd be glad to do it. But the bank examiner will be here next week and if he saw a note signed by two minors and secured by a mortgage on a pack train of burros, I'd have a lot of explaining to do. But I'll think it over. You come back tomorrow."

The boys felt that this was nothing more than a courteous brush-off. But Mr. Campbell's description of the way a bank examiner would react to such a loan was very convincing.

"If he had said yes," Frank asked, "what would you have done?"

"I had that much figured out," Roy answered. "We'd have saddled my ponies and started looking for burros."

"All right, let's do that. We haven't anything pressing, and it will be at least a way to pass a horrible day."

The two ponies, Toby, a dark gray, and Billy, a trim built sorrel, were in the corral back of Roy's home. Mrs. Barnett was at the telephone when Roy entered. He heard her say, "I can't imagine." Then after a moment in which she seemed to be listening intently, she said, "I'll come up and talk with you."

Roy went to his room to put on his outdoor clothes and riding boots. When he came out, his mother was standing in the middle of the room, a puzzled expression on her face. "Going out, son?" she asked.

Roy thought there was a queer restraint in her voice as he replied, "Yes, Mother. Frank Mathews and I are going for a ride. I want to see how my burros have stood the winter." He kissed her and went out to the back yard.

Half an hour later, Mrs. Barnett was seated in Mr. Campbell's private office, listening to the story of Roy's attempt to borrow two hundred dollars to increase the number of animals in his pack train.

"It seems odd to me. I wonder what he has in mind?" she said. "Of course, you did not lend him the money."

Campbell shook his head. "No. But I didn't close the door on him. I wanted a chance to talk with you. You know, Alice, something of the struggle I had to get started. If I could have had a little help when I left high school, it would have saved me years of painful effort. Most boys today are looking for an easy way to live. They don't want to face the struggle and toil that is the only sure way to success. Frankly, I am intrigued by the plan the boys seem to have worked out. I know Charley Woodruff, the superintendent of the Legal Tender. A hard man, who will drive a close bargain, but an honest one. He will give Roy and Frank a fair chance. I know that you can't afford to gamble on Roy's future, but I don't want to take the responsibility of blocking his first effort to get a university education. I thought you should know about this."

"Then you think, Jim, that I should loan him the money?"

"Positively no. Such a loan would be bad psychology. If you agree with me, I will tell Roy that I have arranged to make the loan personally, taking a note signed by both boys. If I am right in my judgment, they will pay the note. If my judgment is wrong, at least my conscience will be clear."

Mrs. Barnett extended her hand. "I didn't know we had bankers like you any more, Jim. Make your loan in your own way. If Roy doesn't pay, I will."

"Bankers can't always follow their inclinations, Alice. But this time I'm going to do as my heart prompts rather than follow the cold rules of business. Thank you for coming to the bank."

As Mrs. Barnett walked back home, she saw the two boys riding up the main street on their way to the open range where several small herds of burros grazed. The two ponies were enjoying the canter as much as the boys did. Toby bucked a few jumps just to let off steam. Roy reined him up sharply. "Better save that stuff for what's ahead," he advised. "You'll need all the go-some you've got before we get these burros corralled."

Frank laughed. "I wish I could be sure we are going through with this, Roy. It would seem like a dream come true to spend a summer in the mountains really making money."

Roy felt the same enthusiasm, but he knew the hardships that were ahead, so he did not indulge in any rosy dreams. "If that banker should have a touch of human kindness and decide to give us a boost, I'd feel very much as you do. The work will be hard, don't kid yourself. But there's a lot of nice things too that no one can describe until he feels the freedom of the open trail and the comfort of a camp under the stars when his muscles ache for a night's rest." Roy stopped talking and motioned towards a small herd of burros. "There's my little pack train. The big

gray is old Colorow, the leader. You wouldn't
believe how smart he is."

The boys rode nearer. The burros recognized
Roy and turned towards him, making the wel-
coming sound characteristic of these friendly
little animals. After a few minutes Roy told Frank
the names of the burros, and something of their
peculiar reactions toward work.

They rode on to look at the untamed burros
that had been bred from animals deserted by
their owners. These were not as wild as those
that roamed the back country. When the winter
snows made grazing difficult, they went into the
village and found food. Roy knew this, and did
not foresee any great difficulty in finding enough
burros to make up the required number. They
found several head that had been broken to
work, as shown by the white-haired saddle marks
on their backs. These they drove in with the
twenty that had belonged to Roy's father. When
the little herd was finally in the corral, the boys
learned that only five of the forty they had rounded up could be called unbroken. Roy said that
these could be easily broken to pack.

The day had been a busy one. The boys decided that they would not start breaking the burros until they had the final answer from the bank. But the plan for a summer's work seemed so attractive that fear of not getting enough money to make a start was almost unbearable. To an older person the suspense would have meant a sleepless night, but with the confidence of youth, both boys slept as peacefully as they ever did.

Shortly after the bank opened in the morning, they went in to see Mr. Campbell, and immediately felt the encouragement in the banker's voice in greeting them. He pushed a note across the table, and, when they signed it, he gave them a few words of advice. "You'll find Woodruff to be a man of his word. The trail to his mine has been blocked with snow for six months; that's why he mentioned the timber. That is what he needs most right now."

A few minutes later the boys looked at each other with amazed joy as they stood on the street just outside the bank. Frank was the first to speak. "Roy, perhaps you better pinch me. Maybe I'm in a trance."

Roy held up a roll of bank notes. "The sight of

this would wake up a dead man. Let's go down to Mac Dermott's and get those saddles we bought."

On the way down to the secondhand store, Frank again brought up the subject of Roy going to Carson to make sure they could get the job of packing ore before they stuck their chins out any further.

"I've been mulling that over," Roy replied. "I've reached the conclusion that it would be best for us to take our pack train up there. What the banker told us about the trail having been blocked for six months I know to be the fact. Probably nothing would please this man Woodruff so much as to have us pack some timber to the mine right away."

"You're right as two rabbits, Roy. I see your point. The sooner we can get up to that mine and pack some of the timber he needs the better."

Roy nodded complete agreement. "Let's go."

Mac Dermott had a rickety old wagon which he loaned the boys for the purpose of hauling the saddles and blankets to the corral. There were a number of small rope halters tied to the saddles. These Roy had noticed the day before. He gave one to Frank. "We'll begin halter breaking these untamed burros right away. I'll rope one and, when he chokes himself down, you can slip this halter onto his head."

Roy expertly tied a honda in one end of the long lash rope and drew the end through to form a loop. Frank watched Roy's fingers as the knot was tied. "Cowboy stuff, huh?"

"Not exactly. But one has to know how to handle a rope if he's going to pack. We can get along with what experience I've had." Roy flipped the loop over the head of one of the burros and took a couple of turns around the snubbing post in the center of the corral. The burro ran until the rope snapped tight, bucked a few times in an attempt to get the loop over his head, then sat back, pulling with all his might against the rope.

The loop tightened, closing the animal's throat and shutting off the air. The struggle was a short one. The body of the choking burro swayed from side to side. "Get ready to put the halter on him the instant he falls," Roy told Frank.

"O.K. I'll do my best."

The burro tumbled over on the ground. Roy loosened the rope in order to relieve the torture.

The burro sprang to its feet, whirled and kicked Frank before the boy could get out of the way.

Frank got up, rubbing the spot where the little hoofs had hit him. He looked reproachfully at Roy. "You knew he'd do that, didn't you?"

Roy shook with laughter. "That kick may be valuable. You know now that the back end of a burro is dangerous. Here, you hold the rope and let me have the halter."

When the burro choked down again, Roy knelt on the animal's neck and told Frank to slack his rope, then pulled the loop loose so that the burro could breathe. When it began to struggle, Roy held it down until he had fastened the throat latch on the halter; then he stepped back out of danger.

"Now what?" Frank asked.

"We'll let the gentle burros do the rest," Roy replied.

Roy knew that the easiest and best way to break a burro is to tie the unbroken one to the saddle of one that has been broken, and let the youngster learn by watching what the trained one does. Burros are smart and very imitative. They will act stubborn and try every possible trick they can think of; but once they become convinced that they have to obey, they become docile and actually try to do what they see the older burros do. This Roy explained to Frank.

During the morning the boys caught and haltered all the unbroken burros. When the untamed burros quieted somewhat, saddles were put on them and each one was tied to the saddle of a gentle burro, then both were turned loose to follow their own inclinations.

The bucking, kicking and fighting gradually subsided and by the time the boys had finished their preparation for the trip, the addition to the pack train was well on its way to knowing how to work.

"We won't put any packs on the unbroken ones until we begin loading ore," Roy said. "The weight of the load will soon teach them more than we can."

That night Roy had a long talk with his mother. He told her of his plans, and Mrs. Barnett listened sympathetically. She was proud that Roy was showing a spirit of adventure and a willingness to work, and work hard.

"Roy, I had a talk with Mr. Campbell," she

confessed. "He has a lot of confidence in you and hopes you will succeed. Of course, I do too. He thinks Mr. Woodruff will do the right thing by you when he finds out that you really intend to do the work right."

"Mother, you know I'm not over-confident, but I intend to do the best I can, and so does Frank."

Chapter 2

THE FOLLOWING DAY the boys saddled the burros, packed the extra saddles and their camp outfit on them and moved out of Del Norte to a grassy park, three miles up the Rio Grande.

"We'll get the feel of the trail," Roy said, "and arrange the packs. Tomorrow we'll be ready to get a good start and go places. If you want to stick around camp, you'll find plenty to do while I'm gone to town to buy the rest of the supplies we'll need on the way to Carson."

"I'll say there's plenty to do," Frank replied. "I'm beginning to see that I've got to study harder to learn the practical things than I ever did in school. Do you know, Roy, I don't care if I don't crack a book for a long time."

"Don't worry, you won't—at least not the kind you're thinking about," Roy told him. "Well, here we go! I'll be back before dark," and he rode off on Toby, driving two gentle burros ahead of him.

Shortly after sundown, he returned to camp to find Frank studying the list of names he had copied from the saddles. He greeted Roy with an amused grin. "I never would have suspected you of being a religious lot. But judging from the names you gave your burros you must be. I see one is named Beecher, and I notice the Mormons are not neglected. One is called Brigham."

"Right," Roy admitted. "But you'll find about the same number of famous scouts too. There are Carson, Bridger, Bent and Custer; even the Indians are not overlooked. The trail leader, you already know, is named Colorow. That fat lazy one is Sitting Bull. The skinny one is Lazarus and

those two that are always scrapping are Esau
and Jacob. I like nice substantial names and I
think the burros do too," he laughed. "Have you
been practising those pack hitches I showed
you?"

"Yes. Most of them are not hard to tie. But I
can't seem to get the hang of the diamond hitch."

"Never mind about that now. You won't need
it for a long time. Get the tie-rope hitches fixed
in your mind. That's all we'll be using in packing ore. A simple timber hitch will do for the
timber and stulls. When we get a chance to
pack merchandise, I'll show you the keg and
box hitches."

The boys were up before daylight next morning. When the sun peeped over the crest of the
Sangre de Cristos, the long line of burros was
moving up the road towards the mining camp of
Carson. Colorow stepped out bravely, his black-
tipped ears pointed towards the back range. He
held to a gait that should cover twenty miles
before time to camp for the night.

As they rode behind the train, Roy identified
the burros by name in order to help Frank in
picking the right saddles the following morning.

The route lay along the south bank of the Rio Grande River, which at this time of year, early June, was running bank to bank full of water from the melting snow. It was an ideal morning for the start, and the boys felt the surge of happy anticipation. Their hopes of success were high. The smell of earth stirring under the pressure of swelling bulbs and growing roots inspired them both with energy.

Bluebirds flitted among the fresh green leaves of the aspens. A friendly robin called cheerily from a fence post. From the safety of his perch, high up on the trunk of a dead spruce, a yellow-hammer rapped out a message of good cheer.

"At the rate the burros are stepping out," Roy said, hopefully, "we'll be catching a mess of trout from Clear Creek tomorrow."

"There must be lots of trout in the river here," Frank replied.

"There are, but we haven't time to stop and seine minnows for bait and at this time of year the water is too roily for flies. The spring freshets may have run off from the valley of Clear Creek, and if so, we can catch all we want with flies," Roy explained.

The burros, getting warmed up, broke into a trot. "Roll out, Roll OUT," Roy shouted joyfully. "The trail is open and the grass is green on the Lake Fork. We'll give you burros a few days' rest when we get there."

About four o'clock in the afternoon, Colorow turned off the road into a little park where the grass was good. He gave Roy a quizzical look, as though he asked, "How about camping here?"

This sent Frank into a roar of laughter. "If that isn't smart! How do you suppose he knows it's time to make camp?"

"Burros are plenty smart. Probably Colorow has camped here before. If not, he's tired and thought this would be a good spot. Anyway, I'm hungry. Let's get the saddles off as quickly as we can before the burros scatter to graze."

Roy took the saddle off the first burro he came to, shook out the cinch and breeching, then laid it on the grass, and spread the blanket smoothly over it. "Put the saddle you have just taken off on top of this one," he directed Frank, "and put the blanket on it. When we get a pile of five, we'll start another one. That makes them easy to

handle and the blankets will dry smooth. If we are careful about this each day, there will be no sore backs among the animals."

Frank stood back and watched Roy start a pile of saddles. "It looks easy but I'm awfully awkward. When I make mistakes, tell me."

"Once you get the habit of doing a thing the right way, it's easier than just throwing the stuff down in the mud," Roy answered.

"Sure thing, but I'm worse than stupid at this sort of work. I've never camped out much and you'll have to show me the ropes," Frank replied, apologetically.

"You'll soon learn. Camping is the most natural way to live—if you don't spoil it with a lot of bothersome rules. Dad used to tell me, 'Do what comes natural and easy. Use your head and don't make work out of what should be play.'"

"Your dad must have been quite a guy. I'd never suspected it from what I've seen of his offspring."

"So, for that one I stuck my chin out," Roy admitted, grinning.

The evening before the trip, Roy had stopped at a market in Del Norte and bought some steaks.

These they broiled over glowing aspen coals. Frank spread a canvas on the grass for a table, and they thoroughly enjoyed their first meal in the open. After supper Roy took the axe and went back into the forest to cut a small spruce tree, which he dragged into the camp. He began lopping off the long feathery branches until he had a large pile, then he took a sharp jackknife and began trimming the softest twigs from the branches.

"Now what?" Frank asked.

"Bring that aspen log over here onto this level spot and I'll show you."

Frank brought the log and laid it on the spot indicated. Roy threw an armful of the twigs on the ground and began to set them on end—butt down and the feathery tops up. Carefully he placed each twig, making a row wide enough for a double bed. Then he set another row against the first one, making a level mattress a foot deep. Frank soon caught the idea and went on with the work while Roy cut more twigs. When the mattress of twigs was large enough, they spread a canvas over it and made up a bed, covering it by folding the other end of the can-

vas back so that the blankets were fully protected in case of rain.

"One thing more, then we'll be through for
today," Roy said. He took a gallon jug from one
of the boxes, put a quart of flour in it, added a
cake of dry yeast, then filled the jug with water
and vigorously shook the contents.

"That looks like pancakes for breakfast,"
Frank speculated.

"Not yet. But tomorrow every time the burro
that carries that jug takes a step he'll be helping
make sourdough bread for us. Jiggling the yeast
will make it ferment and the heat of the sun will
make the batter sour. In about two days it will
be ready to use. Come on, let's try our new bed."

Frank stretched out between the blankets and
sighed. "Gosh, this is the best bed I ever crawled
into. Something tells me that I'm going to enjoy
myself in spite of poor company."

Roy landed a good hard spank. "You get cocky
and you'll eat your own cooking."

"Oh no, not that, please," Frank exclaimed,
and the two dropped off to sleep.

The tinkling of Colorow's bell woke them
shortly after daylight, as the burros got up and

started to graze. Frank rolled out and lighted the shavings of dry aspen he had whittled the evening before. As soon as these caught, he piled on dry wood. In a few minutes a bright fire roared.

Roy sat up with his long arms looped over his knees. "I wondered what I brought you along for. Now I understand."

"Don't get any wrong ideas," Frank came back. "I'm not going to get the habit. But the thought of setting a match to those dry kindlings was just too much to pass up."

"All right. All right. But as long as you're up, put the coffee pot on and start cooking breakfast while I fold these blankets."

Shortly after noon that day, the boys discovered that the trip to the mine, where they hoped to get steady employment, was not to be entirely a joy ride. The morning had been uneventful. Frank asked many questions about the work they were going to do. Roy answered them as well as he could. They had left the main traveled road to Lake City and were now following a cut-off trail by way of South Clear Creek Valley. Com-

ing out of a spruce forest, they saw a yellow line
of water that swept down from the melting snow-
banks above timberline and filled the channel.

Roy knew the ford and had dared it many
times but never before during the spring runoff.
He cantered ahead of the burros for a closer look,
which didn't make him feel any better. The
heavy water, while little more than knee deep,
rushed down the channel at such speed that it
scared the burros. Roy doubted if the wary little
animals would attempt to ford it. He motioned
to Frank to let the burros walk slowly and for
him to come for a look at the stream.

Frank's face fell. "We can't cross that," he remarked.

"I'm not too sure," Roy said. "Colorow has had
a lot of trail experience. I believe if I put a halter
on him and ride ahead that he will go through.
If he does, the others will follow. It's worth trying. We've got to get to Carson before some
other outfit grabs that job."

"Suppose we wait and cross the creek in the
morning when the water is lower," Frank suggested.

"And perhaps lose our chance for a summer's
work?" Roy snapped back. "After all, we can't

give up at the first obstacle. This doesn't look
nearly as impossible to me as the bank deal did,
and that worked out."

"All right," Frank agreed. "You know a lot
more about what the burros can stand than I
do, but that ford looks dangerous to me."

Roy made no reply. He was slipping a halter
over the long ears of the leader. He got back on
Toby and led Colorow towards the ford. "Drive
the others in as close as you can," he directed,
and touched Toby with his spurs.

The pony plunged in fearlessly, and though
Colorow hung back a little, he followed. Roy felt
the force of the current as it pushed Toby down
stream. But the mountain-raised pony turned his
breast against it and a moment later was in quiet
water near the opposite bank. The burros crowded in close behind him.

Roy turned in the saddle to look back. The
older burros had confidence in their leader, and
were crossing safely. But as Roy's eyes ran back
over the line, he saw something that caused his
heart to miss a beat. In his anxiety about the
crossing, he had forgotten to untie the halter
rope on one of the wild burros that refused to
stay in the trail. All the others had given up their

independence, but Muggins, a fine little black
stallion, still fought for his liberty. And in order
to make sure that he did not break away and go
back to the Del Norte range, the boys had kept
him tied to the saddle on Beecher, one of the best
and stoutest burros in the train.

Beecher and Muggins were now behind the
other animals and had just stepped into the
stream. It was too late to attempt to stop them.
Frank was doing as he had been told to do,
crowding the burros, forcing them to follow
Colorow.

More than half of the train was clambering
safely up the bank, and Roy began to hope that
wise old Beecher might manage to get across in
spite of his handicap when Muggins took a stubborn streak and sat back on his hind legs, pulling
Beecher off his feet in the middle of the current.
Thus the wild burro not only threatened the lives
of both animals, but as Beecher carried the two
mess boxes in which the cooking outfit and food
had been carefully stored, his loss would be dis-
astrous. If Beecher were carried down into the
canyon below the ford, the whole venture would
be delayed, if not ruined.

Roy turned Colorow loose and jerked down the rope he had tied to his saddle horn. "Keep above the ford," he yelled to Frank. "Don't let your pony get tangled up in that mess."

Beecher was kicking, plunging and trying to free himself from the rope that kept pulling him under each time he succeeded in getting his head above the surface. Toby, Roy's pony, didn't like the setup. The boy had trouble in forcing him back into the stream. But he managed to get near enough to Beecher to throw a loop around the neck of the burro and tie the end of the rope around his saddle horn. By this time the head of the wild burro had been pulled under the water. Toby was able to pull Beecher out of the current, but was not strong enough to drag the double weight of the two animals to the bank.

All the other burros were across by this time and Frank had come down near Roy to help if possible.

The loop around Beecher's neck had tightened and shut off his wind, so that Roy saw he must slacken the rope before he choked the burro to death. He sprang off and, whipping out his pocketknife, waded into the stream and cut the

rope, hoping to let Beecher get his breath and then pull him ashore. Instead, the instant Roy cut the rope, both animals were swept out into the current and headed for the rough water at the entrance to a box canyon.

The boys now saw that unless they could free Beecher from the weight of the wild burro, both animals would be lost. They ran along the shore, making frantic efforts to get hold of Beecher's halter, but failed. Roy ran the last possible yard above the swift water, at the entrance of the canyon, and risked his own life by wading in until the weight of the current swept him off his feet. The bodies of the two burros were carried past him, and but for the help Frank gave him by plunging into the stream and grabbing him by the arm, Roy would have been drowned. At the moment both boys were too shocked and overcome by their efforts to realize fully the extent of the disaster.

They fell on the bank, struggling for breath. Frank had not taken much water into his lungs, and was the first to sit up and look down towards the canyon. He saw one of the mess boxes that had been packed on Beecher come loose, and smash on a rock at the edge of the stream. He got up and staggered along the bank, hoping to rescue some of the contents. He picked up a frying pan, the one utensil left to them of their complete outfit. Their dutch oven and all the other iron cooking equipment, as well as the lighter implements and dishes, had been carried away.

Roy was sitting up, coughing violently when Frank came back. It was several minutes before the boys recovered enough to think clearly. Soon Roy stood up, breathing more easily but looking very discouraged. "We're only one day's travel from the mine, so we can't replace old Beecher. He was one of our most dependable burros. The loss of our cooking outfit and supplies isn't nearly as bad. That jug of sourdough that I packed on Colorow will have to do us for food until we can get to a store and buy grub."

"We might borrow a few things at the mine," Frank suggested.

"Sure," Roy admitted, "but this man Woodruff might think that if we can't get along on an open trail without losing our cook oufit, we aren't very dependable. No, I'd rather go hungry for a day or two than tell anyone about our loss."

Chapter 3

THE INCIDENT CAST a shadow over the rest of the trip. Both boys thought more soberly of how easily disaster might overtake them. They realized that one or both of them might have lost their lives at the ford. While nothing more was said about the loss of the burros, they were much more alert to possible danger.

The following morning the boys left the burros to fill up on the rich grass in the Lost Trail Valley and went up to Carson to see about the job. Charley Woodruff was a quiet capable man who knew the details of the mining business. He was in his office, going over some laboratory sheets with his assayer, a young mining engineer by the name of Catron.

Roy introduced himself and handed Woodruff the clipping he had cut from the Lake City paper. "We came to see about this job of packing."

Woodruff sized the boys up for a moment. "Where is your stock?" he asked.

"We have a train of thirty-eight burros about a mile down the valley," Roy told him.

"Have you had experience?" was the next question.

"Yes. I think we can handle most anything you have to pack, if you will give us a chance to prove it."

"Are you prepared to give bond for the performance of the work?"

Roy's heart sank. It had not occurred to him that a bond might be required. But he had sense enough to answer frankly. "No sir, not in bankable security. But we would be willing to have you hold back part of our check each month if that would be sufficient protection."

Catron turned his face away to hide a smile, and Roy saw an amused glint in the eyes of the older man.

"I have just had an interview with a man who has a mule outfit over on the Silverton side of the range," Woodruff explained. "He can't start work until next week. If you would care to see what you can do in the meantime, I might consider giving you a trial."

This was a different reception from the one the boys had hoped for, but it was a chance and they accepted.

"How much can your burros pack?" Woodruff asked.

"I suppose the sacks weigh about one hundred pounds each?" Roy queried.

Woodruff nodded.

"We will load two sacks to the burro to start with," Roy continued. "After the backs of the animals get toughened up, we can load three part of the time. I wouldn't want to agree to load that much every day."

"That's fair enough. What we most need right now is timber for the mine. Could you bring up a load of lagging tomorrow?"

The man's eagerness encouraged Roy. "If it would be any accommodation, we can beat that. Our burros are down on Lost Trail Creek. We can get them and bring a load of lagging up this afternoon."

Roy's quick response pleased Woodruff. "That's a deal. I had the timber cut last summer but an early snow blocked the trail. You'll find it piled up on the east side of Ironbed Flats. If you can manage to bring a few stulls, too, that will be a big help."

"Thanks for the chance," Roy said and started to leave.

"Just a minute," Woodruff said. "I'll pay thirty cents a stick for lagging. Fifty cents for stulls."

"We'll talk about that later," Roy said. "We'd like to get started right away so's to get unloaded before dark."

The boys hurried back to where they had left the burros. They saddled them and drove over the range to the Ironbed Flats where they made a hurried camp, and ate a quick lunch of flapjacks made from the sourdough they had managed to save.

It was about two o'clock when the train was brought up to one side of a pile of lagging. The sticks were about four inches in diameter at the large end and eight feet long. They were smooth dry spruce and easy to handle.

Roy put one arm around the neck of Colorow, led him near the pile and took down the ropes. Then he passed both of them through the arches on the saddle so that they hung loose on the front end above the shoulders of the burro. He picked up a stick of timber and laid it against the side of the burro, the large end protruding over the back of the burro's neck and above the animal's head.

"Now, watch where the rope goes," he told Frank. Then, slowly, so that his friend would be sure to see every movement, he passed the rope entirely around the stick from above, then half way around and tied it snugly into the rope between the horns of the saddle, so that a half hitch held it tight.

Frank stood on the other side of the burro, watching intently. "It looks easy," he remarked, and attempted to imitate the movements of his partner. He made the mistake at first of bringing the rope from below, saw that this would not result in the correct hitch and changed it. After a few mistakes, which Roy corrected for him, he succeeded in making a perfect tie, and was much pleased.

The gentle burros were loaded without difficulty. But when the first wild one was loaded and turned loose, the fun began. The burro bucked and ran until he finally brought up under the branches of a green spruce, and was left standing there until the others were loaded.

Because of several bad breaks made by the burros, it was after sundown when the last of the timber was piled neatly on the dump at the Legal Tender. Woodruff came out to check it over. "Not bad at all," he complimented. "Twenty-five of your burros brought fifty lagging; that's fifteen dollars. Ten of them brought twenty stulls; that's ten dollars more. You've made twenty-five dollars this afternoon, which is a pretty good start. Do you want to load ore tomorrow?"

"We'd like to bring up another load of timber

in the morning," Roy answered, "and load with ore in the afternoon. That will get us down to the end of the wagon road in time to fix us up a camp in the evening."

Woodruff was well satisfied with what the boys had accomplished in delivering the much needed timber so quickly. "All right," he said, "We'll play it your way for a while and see how it works out."

The boys were too tired to cook more flapjacks that night and, as soon as the burros were unsaddled and turned loose to graze, they lay on the ground resting. Frank said, "Do you realize that we made more in this one afternoon than I'd have made in a week working for wages?"

"I know. It looks like falling into a gold mine, I'll admit that. But there's no way we can see ahead as to what will happen when that man with the mule outfit comes for the job," Roy answered back. "I know Mr. Woodruff is pleased with the way we jumped into the job today. I think we have an even break for a contract. And, you know, I had a few minutes talk with Mr. Catron, the assayer. I told him that I wanted to go to Colorado School of Mines this fall. He seemed interested and said he hoped I could make it."

Frank unrolled the bed and dropped down on it. "I sure don't need any spruce twigs to make me sleep tonight."

The boys were pleased next morning to find that the burros had been quieted by the previous day's work and were much easier to handle. Even the untrained animals stood still while they were saddled.

Frank baked sourdough pancakes in the frying pan taken from the pack on the dead burro. Shortly after sunup they began loading timber. The change in the disposition of the burros made the work of loading go faster. Frank, too, was rapidly catching on. By ten o'clock they were unpacking at the mine, when Woodruff came out on the dump.

"You kids sure get out in the morning," he said good-naturedly.

Roy thought Woodruff's attitude was favorable. "Which would you rather have us do, make another trip for timber or take a load of ore to the wagon road? We'll do whatever you say."

"You have done so well with the lagging and

stulls that we'll have enough to last until you come up tomorrow. On the other hand, the ore house is so crowded that my ore sorters haven't room to work. I think you better load ore."

Frank found it more difficult to place the ore sacks correctly on the burros, but the train was finally loaded. Each burro carried a load of two hundred pounds, which at the rate of four dollars per ton would add sixteen dollars to their earnings, already nearing fifty dollars.

"If we could only be sure of steady work," Frank said as they were unloading the ore on the platform at the end of the road, "I think I'd turn handsprings or do something to celebrate."

"We made a smart move," Roy replied, "when we brought the burros here instead of one of us coming up to ask for the job, like the owner of the mule outfit did. I've been doing a little figuring, Frank. If we could make two trips up, loaded with timber and one down here with ore, we'd have all the lagging and stulls that have been cut packed to the mine inside of a week. If we could do that, it might be that the mule outfit wouldn't be so keen for the job."

"You mean that just the ore alone wouldn't

pay them to bring their outfit here?" Frank asked.

Roy nodded, "That's right."

"Then let's do it or bust a cinch," Frank urged. "This is our big chance. I say—do it! If the burros can stand the work. I don't know how much they can stand and I wouldn't injure one for anything."

"They can take all we are able to give them," Roy assured him. "We'll get an early start in the morning and try to get two timber trips in by a little after noon. Then we'll load the ore and let them take it easy coming down."

The boys had sent an order for supplies and a few utensils and dishes to replace the ones lost at the ford. The things had been left by the freighters at the camp during the day, so that now they could cook a good supper for themselves.

Frank picked up an axe. "Let's make our camp as snug and comfortable as we can tonight. Tomorrow we'll see if we're as good as we think we are."

"There's work to be done on the saddles," Roy told him. "If you want to boil some spuds and broil ham for supper, I'll fix the saddles. After we eat, we'll make a spruce twig bed."

"Fine. I'm the best cook on the Lake Fork," Frank said. "If I had some cream I'd bake you a strawberry shortcake if I had the strawberries."

"Go ahead and spread yourself, Chef. My stomach can stand anything but those darned flapjacks."

"So, you don't like flapjacks three times a day. Well, I'll show you what a good cook I am," Frank retorted as he put the potatoes in the new camp kettle and added wood to the fire so that there would be plenty of coals over which to broil the ham. While he was getting the things out of the shipping box, he found a can of baking powder and read the directions for making biscuits. It looked easy. "I wonder if I could surprise Roy?" he speculated and looked around.

Roy had taken the saddles to be repaired over to a small building which had been put up by the freighters. The opportunity for a surprise was perfect. Frank worked fast and got his biscuits in the dutch oven before Roy returned. He had spread a canvas on the grass and scattered the dishes about. The potatoes were done and the

ham smelled delicious. But the biscuits were still
very flat. Roy looked over Frank's shoulder,
"What's the trouble, chum?"

"Darned if I know. I followed the directions
exactly. A quart of flour, a teaspoonful of baking
powder, salt and shortening—"

"Hm m m," Roy speculated. "That's about
right." Then, as an idea struck him, "Did you put
in cold water?"

"Heck no!" Frank answered scornfully. "I put
in boiling water."

Roy tumbled over on the grass shaking with
laughter. Frank stood looking at him in disgust.
"Well, wise guy, what's the matter with that?"

Roy managed to stop laughing. "Nothing,
Chef, only you scalded your flour!"

The flat biscuits were soon forgotten in the
pleasure of eating the other food and, except for
worry about the competing mule outfit, the boys
were happy.

They had no trouble in making the extra trip
to the timber, and by the end of the week there
was only one load for the pack train left in the
piles.

The boys were unloading ore at the platform

in the evening when two men, each leading a
string of fifteen sleek mules, came up the road.
Roy saw them first. "Gee, Frank, what an outfit!
It's no wonder Woodruff promised them the
work."

"Woodruff didn't say that," Frank objected.
"He said that he had talked with a man who said
he couldn't come for a week. Woodruff didn't say
he had promised him anything, and he let us
start. We are now in possession of the job, which
is practically a verbal contract. I don't mean, of
course, that we would have any standing in
court, but it is a point for argument."

"I see why you want to study law," Roy replied. "I'd never have thought of it from that
angle."

The packers stopped beside the platform and
sat on their horses, looking at the stack of sacks
and the trim, well-roached burros. "What do you
kids think you're doing?" one of the men asked.

"We are packing from the Legal Tender
mine," Roy told him.

"Who hired you?" the man demanded.

Roy told him that they had been packing timber up and ore down for a week.

"How much lagging have you dragged up with your henskin outfit?" the man asked.

That remark enraged both boys. Frank got red in the face and turned quickly to reply, but Roy saw in the man's question that their extra work might pay off. He made a gesture to Frank. "Hold it, kid," he cautioned.

Roy then spoke to the man. "We've got thirty-eight burros and have been making two trips a day. Figure it out for yourself."

"Don't get smart, button," the packer advised. "If I find you've queered my deal with Woodruff, I'll break you in two. Come on, Dick, let's go on to the mine." The men rode off, leading the mules.

"Something tells me that he's sore," Frank said. "I wonder if he knew he was talking to the best boxer in Del Norte High?"

"Cut the big talk," Roy snapped. "I've no idea of fighting anybody. Men who act tough with strangers seldom do more than talk."

"All the same, if that big bruiser should try to carry out his threat, I'd like to be around."

"Now that I think of it," Roy said, "I'm rather pleased with his talk. His flaring up as he did

about the timber we'd packed told me what I
wanted to know. Catron says that good timber
is getting scarce and that Mr. Woodruff is wor-
ried. If this mule skinner acts as tough with the
superintendent as he did with us, it may prove
to be our meal ticket, because we'll get the job
we're after."

"Shall we take the rest of the timber up tomorrow?" Frank asked.

"Sure. These packers will stay at the mine
tonight, and seeing our 'henskin outfit' roll in
loaded with what timber is left may set off the
fireworks. Anyway, we'll play it that way."

The burros were saddled before daylight the
next morning and taken to the Ironbed Flats,
where the last sticks of timber in the piles were
loaded. The day shift in the mine began at eight
in the morning, and the miners gathered around
the shaft house when they heard the tinkle of
Colorow's bell. The men exchanged glances and
delayed going down into the mine.

Timberline Tom Cadle, a six-foot giant
who admired the courage and energy of the
boys, told Grant Lewis, the blacksmith, "This
I MUST see."

The burros had learned the exact spot where they would be freed from their loads, and crowded in close to the piles of timber. In the week's work Frank had learned a lot and could loosen the ropes almost as fast as Roy. Lagging began to rattle merrily on the ground as the ropes holding the sticks were jerked loose.

The mule skinners came out of the office with Woodruff, their faces flushed. The boys decided that their interview had not gone the way they wanted it. The man who had threatened to break Roy in two, swaggered up beside the timber. "I told you how we treat smart alecks that interfere with our business," he snarled. "I'm going to teach you a lesson."

Roy made no reply but kept on releasing the timber. The man stepped in closer just as Roy had pulled the rope loose on a stull. The heavy stick rested against the burro. The temptation to try a kid trick was too much for Roy. He dropped it in such a way that it must roll on the man's foot. The result was even better than he expected. The man had on high-heeled riding boots like those cowboys wear. In making a quick move to avoid having his toes pinched, he stepped on the rolling stick with his other foot and sat down much too hard for comfort.

The miners roared with glee. The boys could not keep from laughing. The man got up, furious. "You dirty little whelp," he roared, and swung a vicious blow. Again the miners yelled with laughter.

"Ten dollars that the kid whips him," howled Cadle.

"I'll double that," Lewis added.

The mule skinner saw that he had made a mistake. He knew that if he started getting too tough, the miners would resent it. On the other hand, Roy did not think that a fight would help his standing with Woodruff. In fact, he feared that it might lose any slight advantage they had gained by delivering the timber.

"There's no reason for us to fight," Roy said quietly. "Don't think I'm in the least afraid of you. I could probably set you down again without too much effort, but I don't want to do it."

Now that the man had a good look at Roy's strong young frame, and saw how easily and confidently he moved, he realized that he had taken on quite a job. "I'm not lookin' for trouble, either," he replied. "Clear out with your jacks and we'll pay you for what you've done."

"Nope. No sale," Roy replied. Then, remembering what Frank had said last evening, he added, "Mr. Woodruff hired us to do this packing. Our business arrangements are with him."

With that Roy turned away and jerked another rope loose. The movement, more than what he said, settled the matter.

Confused by this calmness more than he would have been by any fight, the mule skinner gave up, disgusted. He turned angrily to the horse his partner had led up behind him, swung into the saddle, and the two rode away with their mules, glaring straight ahead.

The boys finished unloading and went down to the office to see Woodruff. They found him seated by his desk, looking very glum. Roy said, "I hope we haven't caused trouble."

Woodruff made a scoffing gesture. "You aren't to blame. Those packers thought they had me over a barrel, and tried to bear down on me. You see, the timber you have packed up here is almost the last we will be able to get off government land. We must have dead timber or else pack green spruce and peel the bark off. These green logs would be too heavy for your burros to pack. These men saw my problem when they were here a week ago. They knew I've got to have timber pretty soon, so they held back a week, intending to force me to pay an outrageous price. When they came last night and found that you had packed enough timber to last me a while, they tried the strong-arm stuff and tried to force me to sign a contract that was out of all reason."

"You say there is no other fire-killed timber?" Roy asked.

"None on government land. There is a fine body of dry timber over the first ridge to the east of the Ironbed tract, but it's on patented ground. The man who owns it doesn't want to sell it. He's holding it in order to make somebody buy his worthless mining claim so they can get the timber."

"Do you want us to keep on packing ore?" Roy asked.

Woodruff nodded. "Yes. Go on and do the best you can. I'm not blaming you in the least for all this, although the timber angle is serious."

"Do you know Mr. Sam Robinson, who has a prospect over on Cataract Gulch?" Roy asked.

"Yes. He's a fine man."

"He was a good friend of my father," Roy explained. "I think I'll go over and see him. He may be able to advise us about the timber."

"That's a good idea. Robinson is quite a power in this country, and has the confidence of everyone."

The pack train was loaded with ore, and because of the early start they had made that morning, the boys were back in camp at the end of the wagon road before noon.

"Let's get a bite to eat," Roy proposed, "then go up to Mr. Robinson's cabin and see what he has to say about this deal. We've got to think of something fast."

Chapter 4

SAM ROBINSON WAS SEATED on a bench in front of his comfortable log cabin when Roy and Frank rode up on their ponies. He was glad to see Roy and listened carefully to the story of what had happened and the problem of getting dead timber.

"The forest that Woodruff told you about is the one owned by Fields, on the claim called the Iron Mask, about a mile east of the Ironbed," Robinson explained. "I haven't been up there for a long time. Wait till I catch my pony and we'll go and have a look at it."

The pony Robinson rode was a little fat black, sure-footed as a burro, and as the animal knew all the trails, he made good time over a cut-off that brought the party out at the Ironbed in the late afternoon.

For a short distance Robinson led the way through a thick forest of green spruce. In about twenty minutes Roy saw the light breaking between the tree trunks and he realized that they were coming to more open country. Soon the green trees were replaced by those that had been fire-killed. Robinson continued to lead the way into an almost level mountain basin a mile wide. A heavy forest of straight dead trees covered the slope as far up as timber had grown.

"How does that suit you?" he asked.

"It's wonderful, Mr. Robinson. How does it happen that it has never been cut?"

Robinson chuckled. "Two reasons: One is that it's off the main trail, and few people know about it. The other is, as Woodruff told you, it's on patented ground. That means that the government has issued a title to the owner which gives

him surface as well as underground ownership."

Roy said, "It's too bad that Mr. Fields won't sell it at a reasonable price."

"I know, but I've been thinking as we rode along. This might be a big opportunity for you. Fields is an old penny-pincher who runs the store in Lake City where you'll buy your groceries and grain. He wouldn't sell the timber to you at any price. You see, this forest grows on surface ground of the claim that Fields got stuck with several years back. A couple of prospectors found some rich float over here in the basin. They started a long tunnel through a trachyte dyke, hunting for the vein, then ran out of money and had to quit. They owed Fields a bill, and he took the claim for it and got a deed to the property."

"Did anyone ever find anything there on the dyke?" Frank asked.

"No. But I'll tell you about that later. A couple of years ago Fields gave some other fellows a bond and lease on the property but they got discouraged and quit. Fields is ripe now for a new tenant. It looks to me as if the play was made to order for you. The timber is worth a lot more than he would get out of the property, if he'd sell it outright. Nobody would buy the timber unless he had a pack train. This is where you come in."

"We haven't the money to buy anything more than just the supplies necessary to get started," Roy protested. "We started this business on a shoestring and now there seems to be a knot in it."

"Fields doesn't expect any cash. What he would like best is to make a deal with someone who would agree to do a certain number of shifts of development work on the mine each year. He has never gotten a dollar out of the property and he never will unless he gets a combination such as you can offer him." Robinson turned to Frank. "Now to answer your question about the vein. There is a chance of finding rich ore here, but I don't think anybody has gone to the right place to look for it. The tunnel they have started to drive through the dyke might hit it in time, but it would take a fortune to drive it. The last man who tried it told me that it cost them thirty dollars a foot to drive in that trachyte and it's two hundred feet farther to the porphyry where the ore might be found. It's too big a gamble for a poor prospector to take."

"What would you do if you owned the ground, Mr. Robinson?" Roy asked.

"I'd go across the basin and start work as close to the dyke on the east side as I could. I'd run a drift in the soft rock beside the dyke in the direction of the place where the rich float was found. I saw several pieces of it and even the softest crystals were sharp, not worn at all, which would indicate that it had not come far. I believe that there's a body of ore within twenty feet of the surface, if one could find it."

"Then why not sink a shaft at the point where the float was found?" Frank asked.

"That's a fair question. Here's the answer as I see it. Trachyte is the closest grained rock we have in this camp. This dyke holds back all the water that seeps down from above. You can tell that by looking at the bushes above and below the dyke. See how thick that buckbrush grows above the trachyte? Note how thin and scraggy the bushes and trees are below?"

"I see what you mean," Frank put in. "If one

were to sink a shaft above the dyke he'd have more water than he could handle, except with expensive machinery."

"That's right," Robinson agreed. "But, if he were to run a drift south, close to the trachyte, the water would run out through the ditch he would make on the side of the drift."

"I can see that," Roy added. "You think, then, that we would be warranted in taking a lease on the property and agreeing to do so much work each month on the mine?"

"No, I didn't say that. Remember you are always taking chances when you start to develop a mine. No man, not even the best mining engineers, can judge right every time. My idea is, you might take a bond and lease," Robinson suggested.

Roy suddenly remembered how the banker would not loan money to a minor and said, "We can't do that because we are not yet twenty-one."

"Take a five-year bond and lease in my name," Robinson proposed. "Agree to do so many shifts each year—not each month. This would give you the right to cut the fire-killed timber without putting up any money, which is all you're after at the moment. Next fall or winter, after you have quit packing on account of the snow, you can build yourselves a comfortable cabin here in a nice sheltered place and stay as long as you want to work on that drift. In that way you would fulfill your contract with Fields and not interfere with your other business. At the same time you'd have a chance of striking ore."

"Will you be at your cabin for the next couple of days? We'd like to talk this over with Mr. Woodruff," Roy said.

"Woodruff has a right to know what you're doing," Robinson replied. "I'm going to Lake City in the morning and will be around there for about a week. If you decide to tackle the deal, come on down and I'll go with you to see Fields. Perhaps I can do you some good. At least I can be sure that he doesn't stick some joker in your contract that would make trouble for you later on. Fields isn't exactly dishonest, but any agreement he offers needs to be looked over very carefully."

"Thanks a lot for taking time to show us the place, and for your excellent advice," Roy said. "I think we may decide to have a try at prospecting on the side if Mr. Woodruff agrees to take the timber."

"Good luck, boys, and if you come down to Lake City, you'll find me at the Pueblo House."

Roy and Frank put in the rest of the day looking the ground over and sizing up the timber. The trees were straight and clean, just the kind they knew would please Woodruff. The more they studied the situation and discussed the possibilities of the claim, the more enthusiastic they became, and that night they went to the Legal Tender mine for a conference with Woodruff.

The next morning Roy rode to Lake City and spent the day with Robinson and Fields. Roy had met the wizened little merchant once before when he had been there with his father, and had a pretty good idea of the best way to approach the matter of leasing the Iron Mask surface ground. As a result, he finally got a contract that suited Robinson; in fact it was less restrictive than the old miner had expected to get.

After the papers were signed, making Robinson trustee for the boys, he walked with Roy to the livery stable. "There are some very good things about this deal that I haven't mentioned.

You'll be making enough now out of your timber contract so that you can afford to hire a man or two to do the chopping. While they are doing it, you can have them build you a good cabin there —in case you should decide to start your drift next fall. You can put in a stock of supplies before you take your burros out for the winter, and really enjoy the snowy months. The clause in your contract which provides that you may either put in one hundred shifts of work or spend five hundred dollars in improvements, covers a lot of ground. You can build a lot of houses for that amount of money. Any improvements you make, even trails or timber roads, protect your contract."

That night the boys went over the contract carefully, Roy explaining each clause. "You see, we don't actually have to pay anything at all for the fire-killed timber, and only fifty cents a tree for green stuff, in case we should have to cut any, which isn't likely. If we should find anything worth while in the ground, we have four years in which to pay the total of ten thousand dollars. If we find ore, we pay a royalty of ten percent on all ore we ship that runs less than one hundred dollars a ton. Above that the royalty is twenty-five percent. If we give up at any time, all the buildings we have put up will belong to Fields. On the other hand, the royalty we pay will apply on the purchase price of the property."

"It looks like a fair deal," Frank agreed. "What surprised me is that you got such a good one, after the reputation Robinson gave Fields."

"There's a reason for it. Recently there has been a new supply store started in Lake City. When Robinson explained to Fields that we would be buying a lot of hay and grain this fall, it had a bearing on Fields's willingness to deal."

Next morning the boys were up early, grinding two new axes that Robinson had advised Roy to buy. Before noon they were up at their claim, blazing out trails and deciding on the best place to begin cutting.

The first trees were felled down hill into the open space. As there were no large branches to trim off the trunks, Frank said he would saw the logs into lengths as fast as Roy could chop the trees down. The work went on so successfully that when they quit for the day, they had piled up all the burros could pack down in three days.

The next day they changed their work and shod burros.

Monday morning the boys were up before daybreak. Frank got breakfast while Roy rode Toby up the valley and rounded up the jacks. The little animals were well rested and putting on fat. They came bucking and playing into the camp. Some of the older ones begged for bacon rinds.

Frank had not yet learned the names of all the burros and frequently had to ask, "Which one is Jumbo? I have his saddle," or "I've got Custer's outfit but I can't find a burro for it."

"All right," Roy directed, "Just read the name on the saddle real loud, then notice which burro starts for the other side of the corral. That will be the one you want."

Frank laughed but found it worked.

The loading was easier in the new place because of the corral they had built near the piles. This pen was made of light, dry poles and could be moved up the slope as the cutting of the trees progressed.

About noon they reached the mine with a fine

load of lagging. Smooth, straight poles of exactly the dimensions best suited to filling the open spaces between the square sets made of posts and caps, or for making a solid floor above the stulls in the stopes.

Woodruff was highly pleased with the timber. "We haven't had as nice a bunch of lagging as that in years."

Roy told him of the deal they had made with Fields. "We'll be able to give you all the timber you need, and I can guarantee that it will be good."

Woodruff invited the boys to have lunch at the mine. Afterwards when the miners were seated around the dump and the timber pile watching the boys, Timberline Tom Cadle walked down to where the boys were loading.

"I haven't seen you fellows since the day you called that mule-skinner's bluff."

"What you did was a big help," Roy told him. "If that skinner hadn't seen that you miners would take a hand, I might have had to lick him."

"Could you have done it?" Cadle asked.

Frank interrupted. "I just ached to see that big bruiser make another pass at Roy. I knew the exact spot on the chin where Roy's straight arm would have connected."

"Maybe it's just as well you didn't have any more trouble with him," Cadle went on. "The miners know now that you're not afraid of anyone, and there's nothing men around here admire so much as a fellow who does not brag about what he can do, but just lets action do the talking."

"Are you boys going to stay here next winter?" one of the miners asked.

"We might. We don't know yet for sure. We're saving money for college but I guess it will take a long time to save enough for that," Frank said.

"You'd like it up here. We don't have a regular ski course like the ones they have at the big resorts, but the run off the Big Indian hill is some thrill."

"I've heard that you and Bill Hill have run that slide," Roy told Cadle. "If we do stay here all winter, I want to see it."

Cadle grinned. "It ain't much. All you have to do is stand up and let 'em run."

They all laughed at this understatement.

When the burros reached the camp at the foot

of the mountain that evening, they crowded around the platform, each one begging to be relieved of his load. The unloading was accomplished more quickly than usual, and the saddles taken off. The instant a burro was free, he trotted to a rolling place the animals had made for themselves, and rolled over and over to scratch his itchy back.

Frank watched them with interest. "There's one thing I'm sure of. I like to work with burros. They're about the cleanest, nicest little animals I've ever been around." He put his hand on Colorow's neck and scratched. The burro liked this and leaned against him. "I don't suppose you'd like a bacon rind or a biscuit, Colorow? That reminds me, Roy, I'm curious to see how that sourdough you fixed up looks by now. We don't have to have flapjacks though, or do we?"

"I'll make rolls for supper," Roy told him as he began washing his hands preparatory to mixing the dough. He poured a cup of the now highly fermented batter into a pan, added flour enough to make dough—about the same as he would have used for biscuits.

Frank watched closely as Roy put in the other

ingredients—salt, a small amount of sugar and a tablespoonful of bacon grease. When the dough was mixed, Roy scalded half a teaspoonful of soda and moulded it into the dough, and made the whole lot into rolls and set the pan in a warm place.

"They'll raise while we're doing our chores. By that time there will be a fine bed of coals for our dutch oven." Before putting the jug away, Roy mixed a cup of flour and water to be added to the sour batter. "From now on we'll always have sourdough whenever we want it. All there is to it is to keep enough batter ahead for our bread."

"There's a lot to learn about mining that is not in textbooks," Frank remarked. "It seems to me that every move you make has a direct bearing on something ahead."

"You know how it is in football," Roy remarked. "Sometimes you work several plays in order to set up the one that pays off."

"I see what you mean. All this work we are doing now is setting the stage for a touchdown, when we start work on the mine."

While the boys were eating supper that night, two four-mule teams came in bringing supplies that Woodruff had ordered for the mine. The men piled the boxes and sacks on the platform, loaded the ore the boys had brought down that day into the wagons, and left.

"There'll be two more loads to come up day after tomorrow," one of the men said as he drove away.

Next morning Frank learned how to pack boxes, which required a slightly different hitch from the one used for packing ore.

Roy was jubilant. "We'll make forty dollars today, Frank, and if this continues I think we'll do as Mr. Robinson advised, hire a man to chop timber."

"I was thinking about that. If we had a man to do the cutting, why couldn't we go through to the mine with a load of supplies, then come back to our claim, load the burros with timber and take it up before we loaded the ore for the down trip?" Frank said.

"Right! Let's ride up to Robinson's cabin this evening and ask him if he can tell us where we can get a man to cut timber," Roy answered.

Robinson had just come in from hunting when the boys arrived. "I know the very man or men you want. There are two Swedes camped over on Sawmill Creek where they have been cutting logs. I met them in Lake City the other day. They told me that their present job is not going to last longer than this week. They are good timberjacks and experienced miners as well. You can well afford to hire them. Let them cut timber for a few days until they get a good supply ahead, then start the drift we were talking about. Before the snow comes they will be far enough under cover so that you can carry on the work yourselves all winter."

"Could you get word to them to come to our camp?" Roy asked.

"I'm going over that way in the morning. I'll tell Andrew and John what you want. If they like the setup, I'll bring them back with me."

The two men came to the Iron Mask with Robinson and brought their own camp outfit. The boys liked their looks. Andrew had a heavy dark beard, of which he was very proud. He spoke in a gruff, terrifying voice, which entirely

belied his kindly disposition. John had a sing-
song drawl when he talked. They agreed to work
for three dollars a day each, and board themselves, to which the boys quickly agreed.

"It seems to me, Roy, that we're doing all right.
A month ago we were worse than broke. Now
we're making money and have two men working
for us."

"How about sticking with this job and put off
going to college until we make money enough to
carry us through?" Roy asked.

"I've been thinking of that for weeks," Frank
admitted. "It seems to me the sensible thing to
do."

Roy nodded his approval. "I didn't tell you
that Mr. Robinson said he would put in a day
or two looking at our claim, and decide on the
best place for us to start a tunnel. It won't take
John and Andrew long to get a good supply of
timber piled up for us to pack. As soon as we
make up our minds where we want to try our
luck, we might as well let the men build a good
comfortable cabin of logs. They know a lot more
about how to prepare a winter camp than we do."

"Swell," Frank said. "I'm going to get Andrew to show me how to sharpen drills. Mr. Robinson says that he is a good blacksmith."

"If you do that, we'll be pretty independent." Roy gave his partner a slap on the back. "I know something about drilling and handling dynamite. After we get the hang of it, we should be able to make a start as hard rock miners."

During the months of July and August, the boys worked hard. The pile of timbers behind the Legal Tender shaft house grew large enough to satisfy even Woodruff that there would be no such shortage during the winter months as there had been the previous winter when packing was out of the question.

Early in September, a carload of coal arrived and John and Andrew were taken to the lower camp to sack it for packing. Before the last of the coal was delivered, teams began to bring the winter's supplies from the railroad. There was every kind of food to be found in the best stores in Denver. Frank suggested that it might be a good idea to make a list of the articles, so that they could refer to it when it came time for them to put in their own groceries. Roy thought this a good plan, and their list was brought up to date every night.

Light snows fell in October, and the temperature dropped below zero at night. Northern ducks came to the open water of the beaver ponds, and wild geese could be heard honking noisily on their way south. One morning filmy clouds hung over the top of Carson Peak and, when the boys went to the mine that day, Woodruff asked Roy how much longer he intended to pack.

"That's what I want to talk with you about, Mr. Woodruff. We can't afford to get caught here. If we should have a heavy snow, we might not be able to get our burros out to the valley. I think we have packed in about all the provisions you ordered. We'd like to quit November first."

"All right, Roy, but how about next year? Do you want the work?"

"We certainly do; that is, if our work has been satisfactory so far."

"It couldn't have been better. The timber is the best I ever got, and you have handled the fragile stuff in the supply order without breakage. You can figure that you have a job here as long as you want one."

Until now the boys had not had an opportunity to go to the cabin that John and Andrew had been building on their claim, so when the supplies that they had ordered for themselves came, they packed them up and had their first look at the new cabin on the Iron Mask. Andrew was proud of the comfortable winter camp but did little to show it. But John told Roy, "I think we leave you a pretty good place to live. Maybe you like the little joke we play on you."

The boys did not find out what John's little joke was until later, at a time when it meant a great deal to their comfort.

A tunnel had been driven fifty feet into the mountain during the summer by the two miners. The house of logs was located just to the east side of the mouth of the tunnel. On the west side of the entrance, a large, roomy blacksmith shop had been built. The space between the two buildings was roofed over with logs, making a room where timbers might be framed, and where John had jokingly suggested the boys could pile the ore they hoped to find. This made very practical as well as convenient winter quarters.

With the supplies they had brought in and stacked up in the house, together with an unlimited amount of firewood at the door, the boys felt that they could defy any severe weather. The camp outfit they had used during the summer and fall had been brought to the mine. The car and track that had once been used in the old workings on the dyke had been brought down and the track laid to the breast of the tunnel.

Snow was falling steadily the morning the burros were headed down the mountain for the last time. "This place will look a lot different to us when we see it again," Roy remarked, as he locked the door and put the key in the place they had agreed upon.

"I'm glad we're coming back," Frank said. "Do you know, Roy, this cabin is getting to be home to me already. If it wasn't that I want an education, I'd be glad to stay here always."

"Well," Roy replied, "perhaps next year or the one following we will be able to go ahead as we had planned."

Chapter 5

THE BURROS SOON DISCOVERED that they were on the way to their winter home. They playfully kicked up their heels and trotted briskly along the road, making such good time that the train reached a ranch at the upper end of Antelope Park before night. The snow here had turned to rain, and the boys were glad of the comfortable shelter afforded by the ranch. Two days later they reached Del Norte, and the burros were turned loose in a pasture where they would be cared for during the winter. Roy went home, while Frank left on the first train for his home in Alamosa.

Roy certainly had a feeling of power and success when, for the first time in several months, he put on a decent suit of clothes, and went down to the bank. Mr. Campbell welcomed him.

"Well, well, Roy, I see my judgment was good when I gambled on your ability to pay. You have a nice balance, enough to carry you through your first year in the university."

"I've changed my plans about the university. Frank and I have taken a bond and lease on a prospect in Carson Camp. We have put in winter supplies and we're going back there in a week and start work."

The banker looked surprised but nodded approvingly. "A year or two of delay between high school and university won't hurt; in fact, it may help a lot." Campbell stamped "PAID" on the note and handed it to Roy.

"We can't take too much credit for sticking with the job," Roy admitted. "We like the outdoor life. We eat like wolves and fall asleep the minute we roll into our blankets."

A wistful expression came into Campbell's eyes. "It's been a good many years since I've known the pleasure of being physically tired. I'd give a lot if I could look forward to a winter of skiing in the high country and spending my evenings in a log cabin beside a good fire."

Roy grinned. "Our cabin is sure primitive, but if you would like to rough it for a while, come to Lake City and we will meet you and take you to our place."

"I'd like nothing better," Campbell told him. "I'd come up during the holidays but we have a directors' meeting at that time. Later in the season, if I can arrange it, I'll come."

"We'll be looking forward to seeing you."

A week passed quickly. Roy spent much time with his mother, talking about his plans. At the end of the short vacation, the boys were glad to be on their way back to their own cabin. They had arranged to ride up the river as far as Antelope Park with a rancher who had come down to Del Norte for winter supplies. The boys each had a pair of dependable hardwood skis and carried light packs of food for the two nights they would be on the trail after they left the ranch.

Frank also carried a twenty-gauge shotgun and some shells which he had bought to take with him to the cabin.

The morning of the second day they left the home of the rancher. Carrying their skis over their shoulders, they followed a trail once used by the Ute Indians on their hunting expeditions into the Lake Fork country. Some snow had fallen since they had gone down the valley, but it was not deep enough to interfere with walking. They made good time that day and camped for the night under the branches of a silver spruce on South Clear Creek. During the afternoon, light clouds appeared over the crest of the back range and the boys remembered the remark made by the rancher—that the mild weather was not going to last too long. This did not worry them as they would reach their winter's camp in one more day.

Frank cut the branches from a spruce sapling for their bed while Roy cooked their supper. When they were eating, Roy noticed that the coals of the campfire sputtered and he remarked that the fire was talking about snow.

"Is that what that is?" Frank asked.

"Yes. That's only a camper's way of saying that the atmosphere is damp enough to make the coals sputter. But it's a pretty good sign of an approaching storm. I wish we had started a day earlier. That cabin of ours at the Iron Mask would look mighty good to us when this storm breaks."

Snowflakes falling on his face awakened Roy before daybreak. After a breakfast of bacon, bread and coffee, the boys started over the divide between South and North Clear Creeks. The snow was deeper here but not deep enough to make skis necessary. There was a little wind and Roy's hopes that they might reach the safety of their cabin before the main storm broke grew stronger.

By midday, they were well down the slope on the north side of the divide between the two creeks. After a lunch of bread and cold bacon, they pressed on across the valley and entered the last forest of spruce below timberline. The wind was coming up now and snow fell in an almost opaque mass, making it hard to see any landmarks. Roy, however, had been over this trail before, and was able to keep his direction up a gulch that he knew would lead to the top of the main range and come out close to where their cabin was located.

Late in the afternoon, they came to the upper edge of the forest on the south side and debated the advisability of making a camp back among the trees, rather than risk crossing the open space between there and the top of the divide.

"How far is it to the top?" Frank asked.

"Not more than a mile. But what a mile it's going to be! If we can get to the head of this gulch before dark, the snow on the north side is deeper and the wind will have packed it hard enough so that skis will run."

"All right," Frank urged, "you go ahead until you're sure of your direction, then let me break the trail a while. I believe I can do it."

Roy stepped out from the protection of the trees. A gust of wind caught him, pushing his body over until he lost his balance and fell. Here, near the ground, the wind had less force and he was able to move forward on his hands and knees. Frank tried to keep on his feet but soon found that the only safe place was in the same position Roy had been forced to take. In this manner the boys moved a hundred yards up the slope when Roy stopped to rest.

Frank came up close. "We can't crawl a mile before dark, can we, Roy?"

"I've got a plan," Roy answered. "When a lull comes between the gusts, jump up and run towards the top. When the next blow comes, fall to the ground and get your breath."

This plan worked only fairly well. At best the progress was slow, but it was this or a very uncomfortable night, and more than an even chance of freezing to death. The cold penetrated their clothing, numbed their muscles and caused their lungs to burn as if on fire. The constant falling to the frozen ground, from which the wind had swept all the snow, bruised their knees and shoulders.

For half an hour, the boys fought cold and exhaustion until blinded by the snow. Roy decided that it was useless to try to go any farther. He pulled Frank's head close to him and shouted, "The ground slopes away here into the same gulch we came up. We can't do any better than

to go back to the timber. Lie down on your skis and try to keep close to me. I'll go down to the lowest part of the gulch and turn there."

"Looks like we're licked. But it's the only thing we can do," Frank agreed.

Roy placed his skis near each other and stretched his exhausted body along them. It was the most trying spot that he had ever been in, but this seemed to be the only hope of saving their lives. He began pushing the skis along, using hands and feet awkwardly from his cramped position. The snow had not been entirely blown away here and he made fair progress. After a few minutes he raised his head to see how far they had gone, but he was still unable to see the bottom of the gulch.

The skis ran more easily here and the wind was not quite so terrific. Frank came up beside him. "I believe I can stand up," he said, and did so, finding the skis slid slowly and could be controlled. Roy got up and followed his friend. The snow was getting deeper every minute and their speed increased. It seemed to Roy that they should have reached the trees they had left on the south side before now. A new fear gripped him. Suppose they had turned into a different gulch from the one they had been following? They might easily be lost in such a storm. They were unable to see any landmarks and must trust entirely to chance.

A lull in the pressure of the wind made it possible for him to see Frank, who was now a hundred yards down the mountain, and making good time. Stifling the terror that gripped him, Roy stroked expertly but failed to gain on Frank, who was a natural skier. He tried to yell, "Be careful," but the wind whipped the warning away the instant the words left his lips.

There was nothing to do but follow Frank. If they were to become separated, it would be terrible. Another break in the storm gave Roy a glimpse of timber below where Frank was, but that brought scant encouragement because all the gulches along the range were timbered to about the same elevation. A moment later they were down among the trees, partially protected from the wind.

Frank stopped and Roy came up beside him. "Know where we are, Roy?"

"No. But I'm afraid we're in the wrong gulch."

Frank turned and grinned at him. "Not a bit of it. You hit the head of our gulch right on the nose. See that blaze on the tree? I made that last summer when we were running out the boundaries of our timber. We're not more than half a mile from our cabin on the Iron Mask."

The relief was so great that for a moment Roy was unable to grasp the full meaning of Frank's discovery.

"Creepers!" he muttered. "In that case we'll be home in a few minutes. I've got to hand it to you, partner, you sure got us out of a nasty spot."

It now seemed as though the depth of the snow increased with every stroke of the skis. Roy thought that it must be more than four feet deep on the level, and twice as deep in the drifts.

Finding their correct location was a great piece of luck, but it had not come a minute too soon. Now daylight was so dim that Roy actually was on the dump at the mine before he saw the roof of the cabin rising above the surface of the snow. There he kicked off his skis, carried them into the timber-shed and put them in the rack made for the purpose.

Frank got the key from the place it had been

hidden, and opened the door. It was but a few minutes' work to start a fire in the cook stove in the lean-to kitchen. While they were waiting for the room to get warm, Frank went to the wall and lifted a heavy canvas that John had tacked against the logs. "Roy, come here! What a surprise! We sure won't have to bring that old stove down from the old camp as we had planned to do."

Roy rushed into the living room, curious to see what Frank had found.

"Look! Here is the 'little joke' that John and Andrew played on us." Frank pulled the canvas down and revealed a huge fireplace made of rocks that had been taken from the slide on the mountain.

"Well!" Roy cried, "That's the sort of a 'joke' I like. Let's see if it draws." He began whittling shavings. As soon as they blazed, he piled logs on them. In a few minutes a brisk fire crackled in the fireplace—it drew perfectly—and the smell of coffee came from the kitchen. The boys took off their wet clothing and put on dry.

Frank stretched his legs to the blaze. "It doesn't seem possible we're here. I never knew before how good a fire and protection from a storm could be."

"It's sure nice to know we are in where we'll be safe and warm for the winter," Roy replied. "Now, just to show you how grateful I am that you found the blaze on the tree, I'll get you a supper that you'll always remember."

That night, after Frank had fallen asleep, Roy lay in his comfortable bunk thinking back over the trip, and realizing again how near death they had been. The coals of the fire still glowed bravely in the new fireplace. Above the cabin the wind howled and tore at the crags of the peak, but here was safety, and the prospect of a winter of pleasant and interesting work ahead. He cuddled down in the blankets. "We sure have reason to be grateful," he thought as drowsiness began to shut out the sound of the storm.

When Roy awoke next morning, the feeling of protection and complete satisfaction was still strong with him. The wind had stopped during the night, but snow was steadily falling in big, feathery flakes. He got up and started a fire in the fireplace, then went out into the kitchen. From here he could see a short distance into the

forest. As nearly as he could judge, the snow was
about four feet deep on the dump, but much
deeper out in the timber. He made a fire in the
cook stove and went into the storeroom for a
ham.

Frank called, "Hey, why didn't you wake me
up? I'm supposed to build the fires in the morning."

"You'll be doing fine if you get up in time to eat
ham and sourdough pancakes. It's a great morning. I want to get into the tunnel to find out if
the rock is too hard for us to drill," Roy said.

After breakfast the boys checked over their
winter's camp, opening the boxes and supplies
they had left piled in the timber-shed, and carrying the contents into the storehouse. Potatoes,
eggs and other perishable stuff had already been
taken back into the tunnel to a cellar that John
and Andrew had prepared. The boys were much
pleased with the camp, and the way the two men
had foreseen the fierceness of the storms that
were certain to come frequently during the winter months.

"We'll be nice and cozy here," Frank prophesied. "I don't care how deep the snow falls or how hard the wind blows."

"A little wind won't do us any harm," Roy replied. "But, our experience of yesterday has taught me to size things up better and not stick our collective chin out too far."

"That was sort of rough up on top of the range when we didn't know whether we could ever hit the right gulch, wasn't it?" Frank said.

"Plenty. That reminds me of something my father used to tell me. 'The blackest horse in the herd will be white when the snow falls on him.' "

Frank was thoughtful. "That's a very valuable bit of philosophy. I'm going to remember it."

During the fall Andrew and John had driven the tunnel into the hill to where the formation was solid and required no timbering. Roy knew enough about mining to show Frank how to start drilling the holes in which the dynamite would be placed.

"Take it easy at first," Roy advised. "Hold a short piece of steel against the rock, the same as you would a chisel, and hit it with a single-jack." Frank did as directed and cut a small gash in the rock. "Now turn the bit about a quarter of an inch and hit the steel again." Another piece was cut. "Keep on turning and hitting. Try to start a round hole. The pieces of steel are made so that the bit reduces with the length. Unless you can keep the hole nearly round, the longer pieces will stick and you may lose all you have done, and have to start another hole."

Frank worked carefully and in a short time was ready for a longer piece of steel. "This is fun. I think I'm going to like mining almost as well as packing."

It took the boys all the first day to drill the number of holes necessary. Roy cut the fuses at varying lengths in order that the blast from the first holes fired might relieve the pressure for those that followed. On one end of each, he slipped a detonating cap of copper, partially filled with fulminating powder. These he handled very carefully since a jar would explode the fulminate as quickly as would a spark of fire.

During the day a dozen sticks of dynamite containing forty percent nitro-glycerine had been thawing in the powder warmer that the Swedes had made out of an empty oil can. Roy cut one of these sticks into three pieces, which he pushed to the bottom of the hole before he introduced the capped fuse. More dynamite was pressed down firmly on top of the cap, and at last a small amount of powdered rock was tamped on top of this charge.

When all the holes had been loaded, Roy split the free end of each of the fuses and placed a pinch of the nitro in the cut. When all was ready, he ignited them in the order he wanted the charges to explode. Frank needed no warning to get out of the tunnel, and went out on the dump. Roy knew by experience that several seconds would elapse before the first shot would explode, and walked out more leisurely. They were both in the blacksmith shop when the jar of the first shot reached them.

Frank looked at Roy, a pleased expression on his face. "There goes our next step towards an education."

When the last shot exploded, he started towards the entrance to the tunnel.

"I wouldn't go back to the breast yet," Roy cautioned. "Wait until the smoke has time to clear. Nitro gas will give you just about the worst headache you ever had."

"That's right," Frank admitted. "I knew that, but I was anxious to see the results of our shots."

"We'll go back after supper. I could eat the bark off a tree tonight. What do you say to a T-bone steak, broiled on the coals?"

"Boy! What I'd say would make history. But our meat is all frozen hard as rocks."

"Nope. The cold on the mountain came from the wind. Here in the shed it hasn't been cold enough to freeze meat." Roy laid a quarter of beef on a block of wood and ran a butcher knife across the loin. "See, it's just right."

After a dinner such as all outdoors men enjoy, the boys went back to have a look at the breast of the tunnel. Four of the shots had broken to the bottom of the holes. Two had broken fairly well and only one was a failure. It happened to be the one that Roy had drilled. Frank's eyes gleamed mischievously. "Don't feel too bad about it, partner, you couldn't expect to do as well as an old, experienced miner like me."

"No? Well, for that crack you'll do the mucking in the morning," Roy came back. "While you're slaving at that, I'll pick down the loose rock and spot the places for our day's drilling."

"What do you mean—mucking?" Frank asked.

"That's what miners call hauling away the rock broken by the blasts."

By the end of the week, their muscles had hardened so that the boys were able to drill two rounds of holes a day. The porphyry was soft and broke in large blocks, which made the mucking much easier. Frank found that he could load the rock on the car and run it out and dump it in half the time he took to do the work at first.

"Say, Roy, suppose you sharpen the steel and I'll go back in the tunnel after supper and clean out the muck, so that we can start drilling the first thing in the morning."

"Fine. But you're going to learn blacksmithing too. We'll have the first lesson tomorrow," Roy replied.

"Then you intend to work only six days."

"Right. We found last summer that we got along better with one day's rest out of the week. Sunday we'll take it easy, write letters and perhaps ski down to the foot of the hill for the mail or go up to the Legal Tender for a visit with Cadle and the others."

The following Sunday after the chores were

done, Roy went into the blacksmith shop and started a fire in the forge, piling considerable coal around the "duck's nest," the opening through which the air blast is delivered from the bellows to the forge.

"Why do you build such a big fire for the few drills we have to sharpen?" Frank wanted to know.

"Because it's important to burn as much of the sulphur out of the coal as possible before you put the steel into the fire. Sulphur rots steel and makes it difficult to temper."

When the heavy smoke had disappeared from over the fire so that the coals glowed brightly, Roy placed three pieces of steel in the forge and heated them to a dull red. He then laid one of the pieces on the anvil and pounded the bit back, being careful not to flatten the round part just above the bit. "The idea," he explained, "is to leave the main part of the drill in its original shape and make the bit sharp, so that only the cutting part is changed."

As each piece was sharpened, Roy checked the width by means of a mark on the anvil, and then laid it on the ground to cool while he sharpened another. When all the steel had been worked over, he began to temper the bits. "Frank, this is the part you will have to watch closely. See, we heat the bit slowly on the extreme edge. Be sure not to let it get more than a dull red. Now touch it to the water and watch the colors run. Then smooth the surface with the file. See the deep blue moving towards the edge?"

Frank's eyes glowed with interest. "I'm watching every move."

"Look, here comes the gray color we want. We'll catch it as near the edge as we can. In that way the heavy part of the bit remains tough and only the cutting edge is tempered." Roy plunged the steel into the water as he spoke, and cooled it before taking it out for Frank to look at.

Frank worked under Roy's direction, and as he was handy with tools, he soon learned enough so that he turned out several very creditable drills. "I wish I had bought some carpenter tools last summer," he told Roy. "This straight-grained soft spruce makes me itch to build things. I'd like to make some easy chairs and a table to read by."

"Perhaps we can borrow a saw and plane or two from Grant Lewis, up at the Legal Tender," Roy suggested. "Suppose we go visiting. We've been sticking pretty close to the job. A little fun won't hurt."

The cold that had followed the storm had made the snow ideal for skiing, and the boys enjoyed the trip up the mountain and over the range to the mine. The men were all glad to see them. Frank told Grant of his need for some carpenter tools.

"I've got a chest of tools that I gave an old carpenter ten dollars for last summer," Grant said. "He was broke and wanted money to buy a ticket to Montrose. I've never unpacked the chest. He told me it was a complete outfit and that all the tools were sharp and in top condition. I'll sell it to you for what I paid him for it."

"I'd like to buy it if I had any way of getting it home," Frank said.

"That's easy. You can take it along today. Timberline Tom has a toboggan he'll loan you. You can bring it back next time you come up."

Grant opened the chest and Frank saw enough

to make him keen to have it. "I'll not bother to unpack it now. Here's your ten dollars." The boy handed it to him. "I'm certainly grateful to you."

"I've got something that will interest you, Roy," Grant continued. "I got it at a bargain." He went to his bunk and brought an old-fashioned, black powder Ballard rifle, forty calibre. "A fellow here wanted to buy him one of the new smokeless high-power Hornets. He offered this to me for twenty dollars. I'm no hunter, but I tried this gun, and it's accurate up to two hundred yards. The new is hardly knocked off it."

Roy examined the gun. "It's in fine condition. I'd like to have it, but I don't believe it would be possible to get ammunition for it now."

"Load your own," Grant suggested. "There's a complete loading outfit, a hundred shells and a box of primers. You can have the whole lot for twenty dollars if you want it."

"I'll take it. I don't suppose there is anything to shoot up here in the winter time."

"There's a few lynxes and a catamount or two that range down there in the gulch above your place," Timberline Tom told Roy. "It would be a good thing if you could kill them because they kill the mountain sheep."

The boys were much pleased with their purchases and loaded them on Timberline's toboggan. The chest was heavier than it appeared to be. Roy thought it would weigh two hundred pounds. It was about all the two could do to pull the load up the grade to the summit above the Legal Tender. From there down to the gulch where their cabin had been built was a steep grade. Frank thought he could sit behind and steer the toboggan with one foot dragging in the snow, as he had often steered a sled. Roy said he would bring Frank's skis and follow him.

The surface of the snow along the top of the range had been packed hard by the wind. Frank found that he could guide the heavily loaded toboggan easily at first. He pointed it toward the timber and coasted away, Roy loafing along about a hundred feet behind him. The gentle grade ended abruptly in a steep pitch that sent the toboggan down like a bullet. The snow was softer here and Frank discovered too late that he had absolutely no control of the toboggan at such speed.

"Here goes nothin'," he yelled to Roy. "I'm headed for the tall timber."

"Keep in the middle of the gulch, if you can," Roy shouted back fiercely, but doubted if Frank could hear him on account of the air rushing past his ears. If the toboggan crashed into the trees, Frank might be killed. He was sure to suffer broken bones at the very least. The only chance of helping him lay in Roy's outspeeding the flying toboggan. The light skis should run twice as fast as the heavily loaded sled, which cut deep in the snow. If Roy could run near enough to pick up the rope that was tied to the front of the toboggan and guide it out into the open space, he might save his friend.

The skis Roy had on were the best he had ever owned and had been well shellacked that morning before they left the cabin. "It's a thousand to one chance," he thought, as he sped downward, "but I've got to take it, there's no other way."

He dropped the string by which he had been leading Frank's skis and stooped low, in order to offer the least possible resistance to the wind. In this way he was able to choose the smoothest and best conditioned snow, which was a big advantage.

It was a wild ride, with terrible possibilities threatening if he failed to get hold of that rope in time. Occasionally Frank glanced back, his face drawn and white. It was the first time that Roy had ever seen terror in the eyes of his friend.

"Keep steady," Roy called. "I'm going to pick up the trail rope." He was not more than five yards behind the toboggan and rapidly gaining.

Frank managed to lean forward and get hold of the rope, which he held high for Roy to grasp. There was a tense instant of uncertainty as Roy leaned over, his right hand extended towards the rope. Frank reached out as far as he could, and their hands touched as Roy's fingers closed over the rope.

The nearest trees were now only seconds away. Roy dared not check his speed, but let the skis pass the toboggan, then began to turn off to the left. The pressure thus exerted on the point of the toboggan had instantaneous effect. It began to follow toward the open ground and, as it lost momentum, Frank was able to help guide it. Roy now swung still farther to the left and

brought the toboggan to a stop in a little open space at the edge of the forest, not far from their cabin.

The two boys looked at each other for a moment. Then Frank said, "Thanks, old-timer. That was just a bit too close for comfort."

"I'll say so. Next time we try any such kid stuff, we won't," Roy said as he dropped the rope that a moment before had been so precious, and rode across the gulch to where the other pair of skis had come to a stop against the soft branches of a green balsam.

The place where the toboggan lay was nearly on a level with their cabin, so they went on without further difficulty and carried their purchases into the shop. Frank at once started to unpack the chest, while Roy examined more closely the rifle he had bought.

"Look here, Roy. I never hoped to own such an outfit as this. Here is a case of assorted bits and a ratchet brace for them. And a complete set of fine, sharp chisels. Three good saws, hammers, a level, a drawknife and a lot of things I don't even know the names of, let alone how to use them."

"I'm pretty well satisfied with my buy too," Roy admitted. "This rifle has been somebody's pet. The inside hasn't a scratch on it and the lock works as smooth as oil. Here are some loaded shells. Let's see how accurate it is." Roy made a target of wrapping paper, blackening the bull's-eye with charcoal from the fireplace. Then he went outside and stepped off fifty yards and tacked the paper against the trunk of a three-foot spruce. Frank followed him.

"You try first," Roy invited.

"No. It's your gun, Roy. Let's see you hit that cute little black spot."

The first shot was a trifle high, but directly in line with the center. Roy handed the rifle to Frank. "Hold low, it has a flat trajectory at a hundred yards."

Frank shot and hit the bull's-eye almost in the center.

"Swell," Roy praised. "If that cougar Cadle told us about shows up around here, he'll kill no more bighorns."

Chapter 6

T HE BOYS TOOK more interest now in making things. The chest of tools proved a treasure. They hunted for a straight-grained tree down in the fire-killed area, cut it down and sawed off a log twelve feet in length. Frank had made some steel wedges which they used to split out several fairly good boards. These they piled up on the toboggan and hauled to the blacksmith shop, where Frank had fitted up a work bench, set up his vise and made a rack for his tools. He put in all his spare time during the week in dressing the boards to an equal thickness.

Their first work was to make a toboggan for their own use so they could return the one they had borrowed.

"I've been able to shape the boards," Frank said, "but how are we going to turn them up in front?"

"You've done a swell job," Roy praised. "About two feet will do for the turn-up. That much will have to be dressed down to a half-inch thickness. Leave the rest of the boards the way you have them."

While Frank was preparing the boards, Roy put a tub of water on the stove and heated it to the boiling point. In the meantime he cut a block three feet long from a round log about eighteen inches in diameter. To each end of this block he nailed a piece of plank. These would hold in position another piece of the same length as the block.

By the time Frank had the boards dressed down as Roy had directed, the water in the tub was boiling. Roy placed the ends to be turned up in the tub and put an old blanket over them to hold in the steam. "It will take about an hour to soften the wood. In the meantime we'll go up to the old workings and get that quarter-inch round iron rod we saw there last fall. It will make a dandy guard rail for our toboggan."

Frank remembered the exact spot where the rod had been put, dug it out of the snow, and they took it down to the blacksmith shop where they heated and bent it to suit their purpose. By the time this was done, the boards were well softened by the steam, and the boys carried the frame mold Roy had made into the cabin, so that the wet wood would not freeze before it had time to dry. Roy took one of the boards from the boiling water and inserted the end under the strip he had nailed to the round block. The wood bent easily under its own weight, forming a graceful curve. When all the boards had been placed in the mold, Roy laid a weight on the other end so that they would retain the bend when dry.

Frank watched the operation with keen interest. "How come that you know how to do so many things, Roy?"

"When I was a kid, my father ran a sawmill

down here on the Lake Fork. This was frontier country then, and the men had to make a great many things that our friends now buy at any sporting goods store," Roy told him. "One day when I was making a sight for my bow-gun, an old trapper came by and said, 'If you make that knob too high, kid, you're liable to shoot your toe off.' I saw what he meant and from then on I knew how it should be done. You see, frontier men don't criticize a boy much, but when they do, it cuts good and deep. You don't take chances on a second dose, so what I learned to do I tried to do so well that it would stand up under their inspection."

"But how did you learn to drill holes, sharpen steel and all the other things, such as cooking, packing and how to live as we do in the woods?" Frank wanted to know.

"I didn't learn it all at once. At first, this sort of thing was the only education I was likely to get, but I always had an idea that some day I would be able to get to college and become a mining engineer, just as you want to be a lawyer. Anyway, what I know isn't so much. You know a lot more about a lot of things than I do. I haven't forgotten that it was you who found the blaze on the tree the day we were caught in the blizzard. That was good scouting."

"All the same," Frank said, "I wish I could have the sort of training you had."

"Your experience is going to be different," Roy consoled him. "Studying law is head work; it requires the ability to concentrate and work on abstract matters. The things you are learning to do now won't help much in your job, but they are pretty nice to know and you'll enjoy your vacations more if you know how to camp out."

Roy's sober explanation steadied Frank considerably. Until now he had not thought of the present work as anything but an interesting experience, one necessary to get the money he needed for law school. But when he thought of the years of persistent effort Roy had spent and would continue to spend to attain the same end, it gave him an entirely different outlook. He made up his mind to master, in so far as possible, every detail of the mining business. "Who knows?" he questioned himself, "I might make a specialty of Mining Law."

When the toboggan boards were taken from
the mold after forty-eight hours of seasoning,
they retained the exact shape of the mold. Roy
made short posts of iron that held the rail in
position, after Frank had fastened the boards together with cross slats made firm with screws
from the under side and countersunk so that they
did not impair the running quality. When finished, the boys were very proud of their toboggan, and found many uses for it. For one thing,
they could now haul firewood from the timber.

As the snow increased in depth along the back
range, it became more difficult for the bighorn
sheep to get the moss which forms a large part
of their food. On clear days the boys often saw
the animals leaping about on the sliderocks or
scaling cliffs that seemed to be almost perpen-
dicular. It never occurred to them to kill one of
the bighorns—even if there had been no penalty
attached.

One day when the boys came out to the cabin
for their noonday meal, they saw a band of
twenty of the sheep crossing the gulch near
where Frank had recognized the blaze on the
tree. They watched them disappear in the timber

and a moment later Roy caught a glimpse of tawny yellow among the bushes near where the sheep had entered the forest.

"It's a lion!" he exclaimed. "He's following the sheep." He then ran back into the cabin and took his rifle from the rack above the fireplace.

Frank got his little twenty-gauge shotgun and crammed shells loaded with buckshot into his pocket. "Suppose I go around to the left and if the lion should run that way, I might be able to head him off."

"That's a good idea. I'll go up the gulch and try for a standing shot." Roy knew the cougar to be one of the wariest of all animals, possessed of a scent that is unbelievably keen. He tested the direction of the breeze by holding up a dampened finger. "The wind is right," he told Frank. "Be careful not to make any noise and we may get him."

The boys separated at the edge of the clearing. The snow was not crusted here and Roy could move his skis silently. He took care that his shoulders did not touch any overhanging branches, and moved only when he was sure that there was cover between him and the place where the

lion must be by this time. He had an occasional
glimpse of Frank moving silently through the
forest a hundred yards to his left.

As Roy approached the corner of the basin
where he knew the sheep to be, he used all the
woodcraft he possessed, moving as silently as a
shadow and estimating the distance between
points of cover accurately before venturing into
the open. Once he heard a lamb bleat, and
thought the lion had attacked. But since there
was no other sound and no sheep ran out into
the open, he decided that nothing had happened
yet. He was within fifty yards of the place he
thought the sheep to be when he saw the lion
rush from behind a bushy balsam after a ram that
had evidently ventured away from the band.

The quick glimpse Roy had of the great
tawny beast was not enough to permit a shot. He
ran forward, hoping that the doomed bighorn
might take to the open country above timberline, but was disappointed. From off to the left
he heard the little twenty bark twice, and wondered what Frank could be shooting. Suddenly
a fierce growl came from a thicket in front of
him and at the same instant the ram struggled

into the open, dragging the big cat through the snow. The jaws of the lion were firmly fixed on the throat of the sheep.

Roy snapped a shot but missed. The roar of the black powder rifle caused the cougar to loose his hold on his victim and spring into the branches of the nearest tree. Roy quickly reloaded and this time had an easy shot at the head of the beast. A quiver went through the yellow body; the claws of the lion gripped convulsively at the branch of the spruce, then it dropped to the snow in a death struggle that awed Roy. Frank came up and the two boys stood watching the spectacle as the great claws of the dying lion tore at the snow and uprooted a small sapling.

"If he can raise that much of a fuss after he got his death blow, what a fight he would have put up if you hadn't hit just right," Frank said.

"What did you shoot at, Frank? You couldn't have seen this lion from where you stood."

"No. I killed a pair of smaller cats with long black hair on their ears," Frank answered. "I don't know what they are. I saw them sneaking up on the other side of the flock, and I let go— both barrels, at a distance of not over thirty

yards. They're not very big compared with this huge lion."

Roy looked ruefully at the body of the dead ram. "I'm sorry I was too late to save the sheep. Its throat was so torn that it bled to death before the lion fell from the tree. But we mustn't waste any meat." He went over to the carcass and pulled it around so that the last of the blood would drain. "Now let's have a look at your cats. I'm curious to see what you've killed."

Frank's face was serious. "Say, aren't we in a pretty bad spot?"

"I don't know, why?" Roy replied.

"Well, I've read the game laws. There's not only a fine of five hundred dollars for killing bighorn sheep, but there's a possible jail sentence of six months to a year."

"Glory be, you're right!" Roy gasped. "We've got to be able to prove that we didn't kill this ram—if we can." He thought for a moment. "We'll have to make a skinning knife that will get this pelt off without leaving any cuts that might be mistaken for bullet holes. But first, I want to see those cats of yours."

Frank led the way to where his game lay

stretched out on top of the snow. "I made a pretty good shot. This big male was standing right here beside this rock. The female was running over there, but one of those buckshot must have gone through her heart the way she tumbled."

Roy knelt down beside one of the carcasses. He lifted the head and examined the long straight black hairs that protruded an inch above the tips of the ears. "What you've done is to kill a pair of the very worst sheep killers there are in these mountains. These are tassel-eared lynx. They actually kill more sheep and deer than the lions do, because they prey on the lambs in the spring when the ewes are down in the low altitudes. Hunger must have driven this pair up here. They don't usually come up so high."

Frank lifted the long silky hair on the neck of the lynx. "Pretty, isn't it?"

"Sure is," Roy agreed. "I've a hunch that if we take some pictures showing the tracks where the lion crept up on the sheep, and get the pelt off that ram without any holes in it, we can convince the game warden that we are telling the truth, and that we were not hunting bighorns. Come on, let's go to the cabin. We've got work to do."

Back at the cabin, Roy's first work was to find the blade of a worn-out shovel and cut out a curved piece of the steel, which he put in the forge and shaped into a skinning blade before he tempered it. In the meantime Frank had been making a handle out of a piece of seasoned hickory. In half an hour the boys had a first-rate tool. Frank put a new roll of films in his camera and, taking an axe and their new toboggan, they went back to where the ram lay.

"Before we touch anything," Frank proposed, "let's take as many pictures as we can. I have more faith in convincing the officers with the snapshots than I have in any story we can tell."

After exposing several films so as to show the tracks of the killers at the time they first saw them, the boys carefully removed the pelt from the ram, taking care not to cut the hide near the head where the teeth of the lion had torn the ram's neck. They then skinned out the lion and the two lynx, loaded all the pelts and the fine fat meat of the sheep on the toboggan and took their prizes to the cabin.

"There's one nice thing about this, Frank, you are going to eat the finest meat that even the old pioneers ever tasted, but it ought to hang a few days to be at its prime. Tonight we'll feast on bacon and bighorn liver, and that, sir, is a delicacy. Tomorrow we'll go to Lake City and see the game warden."

Next morning the boys piled all four of the hides onto the toboggan and turned toward the valley. It was a glorious winter morning and the skis ran easily. This was the first time they had been down past the old camp and there was much to remember at the end of the trail. They were fortunate in getting a ride with a friendly wood hauler, and reached the little mining town of Lake City in time to see the game warden that night.

Dan Fellows was the game warden as well as the forester. Frank told the story and showed him the head and pelts. "We took several snapshots of the tracks. I left the films at the drug store to be developed. The man said we could get them in the morning."

"You leave the pelts and head here and I'll talk to you in the morning," Fellows replied sternly. "You'll have to give bond for your appearance later. It's a bad situation and you know it. Attempts to get trophies of these bighorns are common, and we have instructions to demand absolute proof of how any sheep has been killed. The lion story angle is the most common one we get. This hurts your case."

The boys felt pretty blue as they walked back to the hotel. "That game warden doesn't believe us," Frank said.

Roy was more hopeful. "The pictures should convince him. If the worst comes to the worst and we have to give bond, I can wire the bank at Del Norte and get a cash bond. It's not a nice spot to be in, I admit, especially with a jail sentence threatening us, but let's keep our chins up."

The day had been a long hard one and the boys slept until late next morning. When they came down into the lobby of the hotel, they were pleased to see Sam Robinson there. He greeted them warmly. "I've been thinking about you boys," Robinson told them. "How is everything going?"

"It was going swell until yesterday," Roy replied. He then told of the killing of the bighorn and of the doubt in the mind of the game warden.

"Don't worry too much," Robinson advised.

"You say you got some snapshots of the scene?"

"Yes. We are going up to the drugstore now to see how they came out."

Robinson nodded approval. "I'll go along with you."

The man who had developed the films was enthusiastic. "These are the most wonderful winter scenes I have ever developed," he praised. "You should be able to sell them for a good price to a magazine."

Roy turned to Robinson. "Would you mind going over to the warden's office with us?"

"Sure I'll go. Fellows isn't such a bad sort, but the department has been bearing down on him mighty hard lately and it makes him cautious."

They found the warden in conference with one of his deputies. He looked sharply at Frank. "Didn't you tell me that there were no bullet holes in the hide of the bighorn?"

"I did. There couldn't have been, since the lion was in a tree ten feet above the sheep when Roy shot him."

"Then what do you call this?" Fellows held up the hide, showing a small round hole in the flesh side of the pelt near the base of the skull. It undoubtedly had been made by a bullet.

The boys looked in amazement. Roy stooped over close to the hide. "It's a bullet hole all right, but I can't see how it got there."

Robinson pushed past Roy. "Let me have a look." After a moment's examination he turned to the deputy. "Do you happen to have a .40 calibre cartridge in your pocket?"

The man handed him a cartridge which Robinson held near the hole. The bullet was unquestionably larger than the hole. An expression of amused triumph showed on Robinson's face. "Give me those pictures, Frank." He glanced at them and chuckled. "You fellows aren't any of you too smart," he joked. "If you'll look at the pictures, you'll see that in order to kill the female lynx, Frank had to shoot directly toward the spot where the lion held the sheep. This picture shows that there is a bush in the way, so Frank couldn't possibly have seen either the lion or the ram. That hole was made by a buckshot, not by a rifle bullet, and it is so small that you failed to notice it when you skinned the sheep. It couldn't have killed the sheep unless it had cut the spinal cord."

Fellows studied the pictures a minute, then handed them back to Frank. "You win. There's no doubt about it; that's the way it happened. I'm glad to accept your explanation. By the way, what do you want to do with these pelts?"

Frank was too relieved to care. "Anything you want to do will be all right with us."

"Well, The Museum of Natural History in Denver has been trying to get a good specimen of a bighorn ram. If you care to send all these pelts to them along with the story of how they were taken, the animals will be carefully mounted and placed on exhibition, with a card attached giving you credit for capturing them."

"That will be fine," the boys agreed in unison. "Will you attend to sending them in?" Frank asked.

"Sure. Just write a short description of what happened and I'll send it along with the pelts."

Roy thanked Robinson for helping them out of the scrape. "After all, what we don't know about woodcraft would fill a mighty big book."

"Don't blame yourselves too much," Robinson advised. "When I saw the size of that bullet hole, I knew that it couldn't have been made by a .40 calibre rifle, and when I looked at the picture it was clear to me what had happened."

~~~~~~

Chapter 7

~~~~~~

THE BOYS HAD HEARD at the hotel that a team was going up to the foot of the trail the next day with supplies for the Legal Tender, so they decided to spend the day writing letters home and reading news of the outside world.

The following morning they left Lake City on a sleigh which carried, besides the driver, a shift boss from the Legal Tender who had been celebrating payday in the village. His name was John

Kemper and he was in no condition to attempt the five-mile climb on snowshoes. Roy dreaded the responsibility of having him for company on the trail but saw no way to avoid it. He told Frank of his fears and they discussed asking the driver to take the man back with him.

Kemper was a short, close built man. His face showed the effects of a debauch, and his hands shook nervously.

Shortly before noon they arrived at the transfer place, and were much pleased to find Timberline Tom Cadle and Wild Bill Hill there, waiting to pack the supplies the team had brought up the trail. Cadle took one glimpse at Kemper, then without ceremony put his hand in the man's pocket, took out a bottle and smashed it on a rock.

"You can't drink whiskey and buck snow," he said to Roy. "If we can make Kemper sweat off the liquor he's already drunk, he may make it as far as your place, but he'd never get to the Legal Tender."

The boys were surprised at Cadle's action because miners have the reputation of being free drinkers. But they knew that these men had learned by experience that whiskey was, as Cadle put it, "no good to a snow fighter."

Kemper managed to get on a pair of skis and stagger up the trail. At first he seemed to be going all right, but in less than a mile he completely gave out and would have perished if the boys had not offered to put him on their toboggan and haul him to their cabin.

"That's mighty white of you," Cadle told them. "It's either that or one of us will have to take him back to some ranch and let him sleep it off."

"We can haul him," Frank put in. "We haven't much to carry and the two of us can pull the toboggan without any trouble."

Kemper made no objection to stretching out on the toboggan and was soon sound asleep. There was a mile of heavy grade to be climbed and the boys made slow progress dragging the load. Cadle and Hill promised to come down the next day to get Kemper, but as it turned out, they were unable to keep their promise because of the blizzard that started that night and lasted for a week.

The following day Kemper was sober and proved to be a pleasant companion. He insisted on doing the cooking, and the first time he went into the tunnel made a discovery that greatly encouraged the boys. Frank had cleaned out the rock from their last round of shots and Roy was getting ready to drill when Kemper came in to see what they were doing. He leaned against the side of the tunnel for a minute, then went to the breast, took the pick from Roy's hand and began digging at a tiny seam in the rock.

Roy had noticed this seam several yards back but thought it to be nothing more than a crack in the porphyry. Kemper held one hand low to catch the particles he broke loose. These he examined as best he could by candlelight. "I wish I had some nitric acid and a copper plate. I could tell for sure whether I'm right or not," he muttered.

"There's a package marked 'Nitric and Copper Plate' in the chest we bought from Grant Lewis," Frank told him. "I wondered what it was doing in a carpenter's chest."

"I know the man who sold that chest to Grant," Kemper said. "He was always prospecting when he had a day off. Let's go see what a prospector's test will tell us."

"What do you expect to find?" Roy asked on the way out to the blacksmith shop, where the chest was kept.

"Nothing to get excited about," Kemper answered. "At the best it's only evidence that somewhere ahead there may be a body of ore. There's not enough of it to amount to anything yet, but I think I can see particles of black sulphurets of silver in that seam. We can soon find out if I'm right."

Frank unlocked the chest and took out a small wooden box that had a neatly fitted wooden cover. He opened it to reveal a bottle, several test tubes and a piece of copper plate four by six inches. Kemper put the particles he had taken from the seam on the smooth top of the anvil and rubbed them with the face of a hammer into a fine powder. He placed about half a teaspoonful of the powdered mineral in a test tube, and poured diluted nitric acid over it. He warmed the contents over a candle until heavy red fumes began to show, then he added water to fill the tube and set it on the work bench.

"We'll let her cook a few minutes. If there's silver in that rock, the acid will take it up in solution. Copper precipitates silver. When we put the stuff in the test tube on a plate, it will coat it black, if there is any silver in the solution."

The boys watched the test with intense interest. When Kemper poured the contents of the tube on the plate and washed it off with water, they leaned over his shoulder to see. Smiles wreathed the miner's face at the success of his experiment. "See that black? Chimney soot ain't any blacker. Boys, she's there! Some place along this dyke you are following, there's a body of rich silver ore and in this camp there is always gold with it."

Frank looked at Roy with unbelieving eyes. "Perhaps Mr. Robinson was right."

The encouragement given them by Kemper's test bore fruit at once. The boys went on with their work with renewed energy and a hope that sometime they might find rich ore on their claim.

Kemper showed them that by pointing their holes toward the seam, the rock could be broken more easily. From then on the boys made the smooth surface caused by the seam the right-hand wall of their tunnel. Kemper told them

many things that made their work easier. He cut
off all the steel and made new bits on each piece,
showing them how to keep the edges sharp without sloping the back of the bit so much. This had
always been a problem with Roy.

The storm broke after a week's blizzard, and
Kemper got ready to go on to the Legal Tender.
"You boys have been mighty good to me. I've a
hunch that I'm going to leave the booze alone
from here out. If you hadn't taken care of me, I'd
have either died on the trail or gone back to Lake
City and then I'd have lost my job. I had a good
job as superintendent on the Gold King over at
Gladstone, but lost it on account of drink. For me
the only way is to leave it absolutely alone. Now
as you develop your mine, if there should come a
time when you need a good foreman, I think I
can qualify. Anyway, I'm an expert timberman
and I'm applying for the job when you need me."

"I'm afraid that's a long way off," Roy told him,
"but if we should strike pay ore, we'll sure give
you the job."

The boys stood on the dump and watched
their new friend climb steadily up the long slope

toward the Legal Tender. "Do you suppose he really thinks that we have a mine here?" Frank asked.

"I don't know whether he does or not, but there's one thing sure: he didn't tell us all he had figured out. Yesterday when I came out of the tunnel for a piece of steel I'd forgotten, I saw Kemper up on the hill above the old workings. He had my compass in his hand and was evidently checking up on the course of the little seam we are following in the tunnel."

"He told me one evening," Frank said, "that the worst evidence there is about the seam is that there is no water coming out of it. He said that the trachyte dyke is impervious and must hold back all the water above it. The pressure in the porphyry must be terrific. If there is a large body of ore in the direction we are driving, our tunnel ought to be draining it now, but the breast of the tunnel is bone dry."

After Christmas, as the days began to get noticeably longer, the boys thought more of the outdoor work that they had enjoyed the summer before. Roy wrote to the ranch where they had left the burros and got a reply saying that all the stock had wintered well and would be in fine condition for heavy work in the spring.

John and Andrew wrote asking if there would be work for them, and the boys were glad to tell them to come up in March and begin cutting timber so that there would be a supply ready to pack to the Legal Tender as soon as the trail was open.

The approach of spring tempted the boys to take some time off and accept the invitation Cadle and the others sent them to join the miners in a day of skiing. Frank suggested that they go the following Sunday—the one day in the week when the miners laid off from work underground to wash their clothes and to relax outdoors. Roy thought this would be fun and they started early to climb the mountain.

Both boys were considered good skiers. They had frequently gone to the public ski course at home, and had seen many experts give exhibitions. They had even run on the courses designated by the Ski Association, and could probably have qualified for one of the nationally advertised contests.

Roy, however, had seen enough of the skill of men who live all winter above timber line to realize the difference between their technique and that of those who only ski for sport. The experience required for country trips through many miles of unsettled country was a far different matter from that needed for rides down a well marked course.

"I feel like a rank outsider," Roy told Frank as they neared the Legal Tender. "Such men as Cadle and Hill can do things on skis that our so-called professionals wouldn't attempt."

"I know," Frank replied, "I saw Cadle packing a hind quarter of beef up the mountain one day. He didn't have a pair of modern sticks with rawhide rings to help him climb, either."

"You're right," Roy came back. "The old-time snow fighters and hunters never carried a stick at all. They couldn't because they had to have their hands free to handle a gun. We'll see some real hill running today. It's going to be fun, even though we'll probably get some hard falls if we try to do the same things Cadle or Hill do."

The miners were seated on the porch in front of the bunkhouse, watching some of the skiers running on the long slope that stretched away towards Lost Trail Creek. It was a pleasant mile run with a natural jump caused by a drift. Most of the skiers went down standing straight, but two failed to keep their balance on the jump and were unmercifully grilled by the onlookers.

"Let's see you boys try it," Grant Lewis proposed. "You ought to be pretty good by this time."

"Not too good," Roy replied. "I'll probably stick my head in the snow below that jump."

"Anybody want to bet five that he can't make that jump?" Lewis challenged.

Bob Murphy, the cook who had just returned from an unsuccessful attempt, took the bet. The obstacle was no more than the boys had jumped on the Wolf Creek Course, and they both went down and over without mishap, winning the bet for Lewis.

After dinner, Cadle proposed that they run the mountain on the west side of Carson Peak.

Murphy shook his head. "Don't be silly. You and Hill know you're the only two men who have ever gone over the jump below the Big Indian mine." He turned to Roy, "Don't let Tom kid you into making that run. The hill is half-pitch, and half way down you take wings and pray."

Frank thought Murphy's advice was good. He had great respect for the skill of the two mountain men who had accomplished the feat. But Roy, feeling that the respect of the miners was at stake, decided to take a chance.

The slope under discussion lay to the east of the low pass over which the boys had packed during the summer. Roy had often looked at the mountain and wondered if anyone could run that slope. Some of the other miners had made the attempt but no one cared to give a public exhibition, so there were no contestants.

Woodruff, who knew the value of rivalry among the men, offered a prize of ten dollars to any one who made the run without falling. As no one questioned the success of the two older men, the betting was all on Roy's accomplishment. Odds of ten to one were freely offered against him, with but few takers.

"Do you think you can make it?" Frank asked, as they were going up the slope to the starting point.

"I'm not certain enough to bet on myself,"

Roy replied, "but I'd sure like to win for the men who are backing me."

Frank did not say anything more to Roy, but dropped back among the others and quietly bet ten dollars on his partner.

For a moment, as he stood on the crest of the Continental Divide and looked down the slope, Roy's nerve weakened. If, at that moment, he had not seen the quiet confidence on the face of Timberline Tom who looked as though this were mere child's play, he might have drawn back. But the supreme confidence of the mountain man inspired him. Roy tightened a ski strap with the same feeling of determination that he had felt when putting on a football helmet.

Cadle was ready first, and stood adjusting a mask made of stiff canvas, without which he would have been unable to breathe against the pressure of the air. Then he took two easy steps and shot over the brink and down the slope. In a matter of seconds he was out on the gentler slope at the upper end of the valley, and was speeding towards the Ironbed, a mile distant.

Roy saw that Hill would follow immediately, and at once adjusted the mask Grant Lewis gave him. The manner in which the experts went down, with easy confidence, gave Roy assurance. When his turn came, he made no boasting gestures, but stepped out over the ridge, leaning forward to keep from being thrown backward by the first burst of speed.

Even with all his careful preparation, Roy had not anticipated the mad rush of air as his body literally fell two hundred feet before he could feel that the snow offered the slightest resistance to his skis. If he had not filled his lungs to their full capacity, he would have been unable to breathe at all. And the vacuum caused by his body rushing through the air would have caused his lungs to collapse.

The timber on the lower slopes was only a brown blur. The peaks beside him seemed to rush past at an incalculable speed. Then, he was down and the skis were running true, in a line as straight as a surveyor could have drawn a mark for them to follow. Nothing Roy had ever experienced even approached this, and yet, at this moment he decided that once was enough. For a few seconds he had stood in the presence of death, and he had sense enough to know it.

A few minutes later he was with Cadle and Hill, who had turned out of the valley and were watching from a short distance on the hillside. "Welcome into our select trio," Cadle said. "Until now, Hill and I have been the only men to run the Big Indian slide. Hundreds have talked about it. A few have had the nerve to try it. But we three are the only ones who have done it."

"Thanks," Roy said. "I don't take any credit for it. I never would have had what it takes to jump off that crest, if I hadn't seen you fellows go first. But it's great fun. I wonder if there is any other slide like it?"

"Not that anyone knows about," Hill put in. "We've talked with men who have skied in the Alps and they said that we were crazy to talk about jumping off there."

The three friends skied back around the basin and then rode easily down to the mine.

When Roy got back, Frank grinned and flashed a roll of ten dollar bills. "I had more confidence in you than you had in yourself."

Chapter 8

TOWARDS THE END of February, patches of bare ground could be seen in the valley below. The snow that had clung to the branches of the spruce all winter slid off. Water could be heard gurgling in the gulches, although the snow was still ten feet deep above the Iron Mask.

One morning Woodruff came down to see the boys. "Spring will soon be here," he said. "We're getting short of grub and the timber pile is pretty low. As soon as the wet slides stop running, we'll shovel the snow off the trails. How soon will you be ready to begin delivering stulls and lagging?"

Roy explained that they had sent for John and Andrew to come up and begin cutting, and that he intended to go down for the pack outfit early in April. "We'll be ready to start packing whenever we can get stock over the trail."

That same day, after Woodruff left, Frank was drilling an upper, as Kemper had showed him how to do, when the drill struck rock much harder than anything he had attempted to drill before. Unpleasantly surprised, he pulled it out of the hole to look at the point.

"Hi, Roy, we've hit something different. Look at this bit, it looks as if I'd hit it against an anvil."

Roy put a new, sharp drill in the hole and hit it a few blows. "When he withdrew the steel, it was blunt. "I think we'd better shoot this hole and find out what we've hit." He looked grim.

Frank went out and got powder to load the holes. While he was gone, Roy, his mouth set in a straight, hard line, studied the rock in the breast. So far as he could see, there was not the slightest change in the formation. Frank came with the powder and Roy began pressing it into the hole.

"It looks very much as though we're licked," Roy said. "If we've struck trachyte, it may mean there's a change in the formation here which does not show in the upper workings. That would account for the failure of the other prospectors to find anything. If that's the case, there's nothing here to find. The rich float found on the surface must have been dropped by an iceberg and may have come from a vein a thousand miles from here."

The shot broke unusually well because the powder had been placed on the face of the harder formation. Practically all the porphyry in the breast was broken into blocks that could easily be removed, disclosing a solid front of trachyte. Roy had not felt so discouraged at any time since they had started work. "I guess we've wasted a winter's work and all the money we put into this prospect."

"Let's go up to the Legal Tender and talk with Kemper," Frank proposed, trying to buck up his partner. "He seems to know more about this formation than anyone."

Roy looked at him with no hope in his eyes but
he agreed and they went up so as to meet Kemper
when he came off shift.

The old miner listened to their description
with keen interest. "How about that little seam
you've been following; was it cut off by the
trachyte?"

Neither of the boys had thought to investigate
that.

"Tell you what I'll do," Kemper said. "I'll go
down with you now and have supper. I want to
see that trachyte. It's exactly what I hoped would
happen."

Roy was surprised as well as baffled by Kemper's statement. "I don't know what you mean."

"Wait till I have a look, then I can tell you."
Kemper led the way down the mountain and did
not stop until he was in the tunnel examining the
formation.

"Good!" he exclaimed, as he scratched along
the wall and showed the boys that the seam actually did cut the older formation. "This explains
why the water didn't come out in the porphyry.
This cross dyke may be only a few feet across
and it may be a hundred. But it wouldn't make

any difference to me if it was a thousand. I'd see on the other side of it if it took the last dollar I could beg, borrow or steal."

The boys crowded close as Kemper drew a little map on the floor of the tunnel. "We'll say that here is the place where the rich float was found on top of the ground." He laid a small rock on the floor and drew a line below it running from north to south. "This line indicates the main trachyte dyke. We know now from the work you've done this winter exactly how wide this dyke is, so we can locate almost to a yard how far those other fellows would have had to drive through the dyke. The cost was prohibitive and they showed good judgment to give it up. When we found that the sediment in the seam, small as it is, had silver in it, I figured that you were not far from the vein, but this theory was blocked by the absence of water. Something was holding it back."

Roy broke in, "I begin to see why you said that you had hoped there was a cross dyke."

"Right. That explains why there's no water coming along this side of the main trachyte dyke. When you drive through this cross dyke, you may hit a glory hole. I may be wrong but I don't think so."

The boys looked at each other, both thinking of the cost. "I wonder if we'll have money enough to get to the ore even if it is there?" Roy questioned.

Kemper was thoughtful a moment. "Didn't you say that John and Andrew are coming back?"

"Yes. We expect them next week."

"I'll tell you what I'll do," Kemper said. "I'm under greater obligation to you boys than you realize. I think the week I spent with you took me back to the hopes I had when I was a kid. I haven't had a drink since that day, and better yet, I haven't wanted one. The boys at the mine got a jug last week and tried to get me to drink. But the smell of the stuff made me sick. Now I'm willing to stake a year's wages on this prospect of yours. If you want me to, I'll take the job of foreman for you. I'll move down here tomorrow and start cutting timber, so that when the miners come they can go right to work in the tunnel. They're good, husky hard rock miners and they'll break more ground in a week than you could in a month. You can go down and get your burros and start packing to the Legal Tender again. In that way you'll earn enough to pay your men.

"If I were you, however, I'd make my pack camp here instead of at the foot of the trail. The grass is better here and you can, by making some changes, earn enough more to pay the added expense. I'll do all the cooking and tool sharpening and cut timber for you to pack. If you strike the ore I think you'll find on the other side of the cross dyke, you can pay me a hundred and fifty dollars a month. If you don't strike it rich, you won't owe me a red cent."

"Jeepers," Roy exclaimed. "If you really think we might find the ore, we'd be foolish not to accept your offer. We took a chance to begin with and we sure ought to have guts enough to take another. Don't you think so, Frank?"

"Yes. But I'd like to add that if Kemper's judgment does prove good and we should find the ore, we'll surely give him a bonus of a thousand dollars."

Kemper laughed. "Never mind the bonus. Just give me the powder and grub and pay the miners once a month and I'll take care of the rest. I'll go back to the mine in the morning and tell

Woodruff that I am quitting. He has a good foreman who can take my place."

It was with lighter hearts that the boys pre-
pared to go out after the burros. The next day
Kemper moved down to the Iron Mask and at
once started cutting timber. The snow was melting rapidly and the lower half of the trail was
drying up. The end of the week John and Andrew came, and, after one day's preparation, they
began work in the tunnel. The boys went in to
watch them drill and were much impressed by
their skill and strength. John was holding the
drill that Kemper had tempered to cut the hard-
est rock, while Andrew struck terrific blows with
a seven-pound hammer, swinging it easily and
with no thought of its being hard work.

Before leaving camp, Roy went up for a word
with Woodruff. "How about potatoes?" he asked.
"The San Luis country is famous for them. I
thought I might bring in a load."

"Spuds cost us seven cents a pound laid down
here," Woodruff said. "We'll take all you can
bring at that price."

There was snow enough on the north side of
the range, so the boys used their skis on the

run down to North Clear Creek, but from then on, the south sidehills were bare. They left their skis hidden under a fallen tree and went on to the ranch where they had stopped the fall before. The rancher was intending to go out to Del Norte within a few days, but was glad to start at once in order to get the ten dollars Roy offered him for their transportation.

A week later the pack train arrived at The Iron Mask. Kemper had been very busy while the boys were gone, and they were surprised to find that he had built a corral of poles in the park below the mine and was just finishing a shed.

"I figured that if you were to make a trip to the mine with timber in the mornings, and bring a load of ore down this far," he explained, "you could pack a hundred pounds more on each burro if he didn't have to carry it the entire distance. By packing this far in three days and the rest of the distance the other three, you would get a ton and a half more down at each trip. That's what I had in mind when I told you that you could make enough more to pay the Swedes."

Roy was pleased by this arrangement. "As

soon as we get these spuds delivered, we'll go down and pack up hay and grain enough to keep the burros in good condition until the grass grows," he told Kemper.

Soon the work was again going with clock-like regularity. The boys found the new arrangement much better for them. For one thing, now that they did not have to cook their meals, they had time to repair saddles and put new shoes on the burros, if any had been lost during the day.

The work in the tunnel progressed slowly. The rock was very hard. Some days Andrew and John were unable to get enough holes drilled to warrant blasting. It was easy now to see why the former lessees had given up trying to drive through the dyke. But Kemper's confidence in the success of the work seemed as unbreakable as the trachyte. "Stick with it, kids," he said. "Nothing worth while comes easy."

Sam Robinson stopped for a day on his way to his own claim. He went into the tunnel and examined the seam that was being followed. "You must be pretty near through this cross dyke," he remarked. "Let's rig up an outfit and make a survey."

Kemper agreed to this at once. "I'd have done that before but I didn't have a hand level."

"I've got one in my pack," Robinson said, and went to get it.

The boys were puzzled as to how the older men expected to measure the distance down the steep slope of the mountain and calculate without the assistance of a transit, but they were wise enough not to say what they felt about the accuracy of the survey. Robinson and Kemper seemed to know exactly how the work was to be done so the boys kept quiet and watched.

While Robinson was getting the hand level from his pack, Kemper made a square of light pieces of wood and braced the sticks firmly in place. He then got a steel tape that they used for measuring timber, and when Robinson returned they all climbed the mountain to the abandoned assessment hole where, long before, the rich float had been discovered. Robinson drove a stake in the old dump at a point where the blossom of the highly-colored quartz indicated that the mineral had been found.

Kemper went down the slope a short distance and sighted back over his square. He shifted it back and forth until it was on a level with the stake that Robinson had set up. "That ought to do it," he called.

Robinson gave Roy the tape. "You can be head lineman. Frank, you hold the end of the tape here over the stake." Roy went down to where Kemper stood while Robinson sighted over the hand level and directed him forward and back until a level was established. Frank measured the distance and called it back to Robinson, who noted it in a little field book, together with the height of the square that Kemper held. The survey took more time than a man with a transit would have required, but inside of an hour Robinson had completed a rough sketch which showed accurately the surface distance and elevation.

All that remained to be done now was to measure the length of the tunnel. As a result of the survey, the boys found that the breast of the tunnel where Andrew and John were now working was only fifteen feet from a point vertically below the outcrop.

"That's encouraging," Robinson told them. "If our theory is correct and the vein does not pitch away from your drift, you'll know before the summer is over whether or not you have a mine. Our survey shows that you are two hundred feet below the old shaft, which is good depth for successful operation, if the ore is there."

The interest of the boys now centered on the driving of the tunnel, but the slow progress day after day, week after week of measuring and drilling was trying their patience. Each evening after the day's work of packing was through, they went to measure the distance the miners had driven during the day. Sometimes it was so little that they doubted if the vein would be reached before winter. Kemper worked harder than anyone. He was up before daybreak every morning so as to have breakfast ready. In the evening he sharpened the steel for the miners to use the following day.

"We never could make it if it weren't for Kemper," Frank told Roy. "If we do find anything, we must pay him well."

"There's no argument about that," Roy agreed, "but we haven't found it yet."

One night after they had turned the burros

loose to graze, the boys came up to the cabin to find that Kemper was not there. No preparation had been made for supper and the miners had not yet come out of the mine. The boys had become so accustomed to the cheery greeting of Kemper and the smell of appetizing food that they felt disappointed.

"We better go into the tunnel and see if anything is wrong," Roy urged hurriedly.

They found Kemper and the miners at the breast working to stop the pressure of water in a drill hole. The black rock that had been so hard to break through was stained by the white mud that was being forced out through the hole.

Kemper's eyes shone. "It looks like we've struck a milk ranch, boys," he joked.

"What's that white stuff?" Frank wanted to know.

Kemper laughed. "That is barium sulphate. The miners call it baryta, and it might indicate that we've struck what we're looking for."

In spite of what he said, the boys could hardly keep from showing their disappointment. They had hoped that the vein would show the rich, heavy gray copper ore that had made the Legal

Tender mine famous. The white sediment that formed in the bottom of the tunnel below the drill hole was not at all what they wanted to see. Wisely they said nothing, however, while the men plugged the bottom of the hole with a piece of wood, and then loaded it heavily with double the charge they usually used.

When the hole was loaded, Kemper scraped up a handful of the mud and took it out to the shop. The others followed him, while Andrew remained behind to fire the blast. Kemper put the sample he had taken in a pan and set it on the stove to dry. Shortly after a muffled report came from the tunnel. It was entirely different from the roar that had been heard from the shots in the trachyte. The boys wanted to go back at once but the men restrained them.

"There's no use in giving yourselves a powder headache," Kemper advised. "Frank, get your bottle of nitric. This mud is fine enough to test without grinding."

Kemper put the ore in the test tube and added a small amount of the nitric acid. The mass began to boil furiously, throwing off heavy green fumes. "There's more copper in this than we found in the ore from the seam," he remarked, "but it's not as rich in silver."

Kemper's judgment was confirmed when he dumped the contents of the tube on the copper plate. Only a thin film of silver nitrate was precipitated. At the sight of this the boys were even more disappointed.

The fumes from the heavy blast made breathing difficult in the tunnel, but no one thought about that as they hurried back to the breast to see the effect of it. The shot had done its work well, breaking a hole two feet in diameter through the remaining shell of trachyte, and revealing a vein of baryta streaked with small seams of gray copper. As far as they could determine at the moment, the vein was about four feet in width and almost vertical.

It was near midnight when they finished taking samples for assay. Both the boys were aware that Kemper, too, was bitterly disappointed, and knew that he had hoped that the shot would show a streak of the high grade ore, such as had been found at various spots on the surface.

"Perhaps the assays will show up better than you expect," Roy encouraged.

The old miner shook his head slowly. "We've not found what I was looking for. This ore will probably pay a small profit above the cost of mining, transportation and smelter charges, but if we had hit a body of that gray copper, such as I expected, you'd be rich men today."

Roy took several samples to the Legal Tender next morning and arranged with Catron to run them for him. The assays confirmed Kemper's judgment. The best sample returned one hundred fifty ounces of silver and two of gold to the ton. Catron figured that the ore would not run better than one hundred dollars, which, as Kemper had said, would pay only a small profit, if any.

"There's always the chance that you may strike better values by drifting on the vein," Catron encouraged. "What you ought to do now is to let me teach you assaying so that you can test your ore every day, and not ship anything but the best of it. That is the only smart thing to do."

"I wish I could," Roy replied, "but I'm afraid it would take too long. I only had one year of chemistry in high school."

"Nonsense," Catron said. "I can teach you how to assay for gold and silver in a week. My helper wants a layoff. Get someone to take your place on the pack train and come up tomorrow. I'll be glad to have you."

Roy talked the matter over with Frank and Kemper that night.

"For heaven's sake, do it," Kemper advised. "I'll help Frank with the packing. It will take the miners a week to get the mine squared up ready to produce. In the meantime we'll be on the lookout for a packer. It's going to take all your time from now on to do the assaying."

Chapter 9

N

EXT MORNING ROY REPORTED at the Legal Tender and was put to work crushing the ore in a hand crusher, then running it through a system of riffles that cut the sample down to less than a quarter of a pound. The next step was to buck the ore on a heavy cast iron buck-board until every particle of each sample passed through a screen of one hundred meshes to the square inch. He found the matter of fluxing the charges much simplified by Catron's methods.

The expert assayer merely put a measure of pre-pared commercial flux in a twenty-gram crucible, weighed carefully half an assay ton of the ore on an accurately adjusted balance and then mixed it with the flux.

When a dozen assays were ready for treatment, they were placed in a very hot muffle—an oven made of fire clay. This fusing operation took forty-five minutes. When the content of the crucibles was in a state of quiet fusion, the molten mass was poured into an iron mold and set to cool. The clear, valueless slag on top was broken off and the lead buttons containing the gold and silver were placed in cupels or small flat cups made of bone ash, and kept at a bright heat until the lead was either volatilized or absorbed by the porous bone ash, leaving a small button of gold-silver alloy behind.

The matter of weighing the gold-silver button on a delicate balance sensitive to one-thousandth of a milligram required practice and great care. Roy enjoyed the work and was sorry when the first day's lesson was over.

"What am I going to do for an assay outfit?"

he asked Catron. "These balances must cost a lot of money."

"If you had to buy them new, yes. I figured that one out before I suggested that you learn to do the work. There is a fine outfit over at the Lone Star Mine. An eastern company bought that property and equipped it with every modern device. Their ore played out. The agent told me not long ago that he had been authorized to sell the assay outfit for two hundred dollars. You can make a down payment to hold it until you get ready to take it. The furnace is an elaborate affair made entirely of tile and firebrick, heavily re-enforced with angle irons and rods to hold it in shape. With a little care in taking it down, you can set it up at your mine and have it ready for use as soon as the mortar dries."

When Kemper and Frank came to the Legal Tender the next day for ore, Roy told them about his good break.

"Wonderful," Frank exclaimed, "except maybe we'll be selling the furnace again for the same reason. Anyway, draw a plan of the building you want for an office and I'll have the logs cut for it

by the time you are ready to move the assay outfit."

Catron helped Roy draw the plans and suggested that he join the new building with the
cabin where they now lived, so that in stormy
weather it would be convenient.

The boys were anxious to make a trial shipment to the smelter so that they might know
accurately how much profit, if any, they could
depend on. Woodruff loaned them enough sacks
for a carload shipment, and Kemper helped them
sort out the ore so that very little worthless rock
was in the shipment. "I want to keep the grade
about to what I know we can maintain right
along," he said.

It was a big thrill for Roy and Frank the day
they loaded their first shipment. Woodruff had
given them permission to take a week off from
their packing, and they got a full shipment of
twenty-two tons to the railroad in that time. Roy
went to the smelter with the ore and Frank re-
sumed the packing.

Roy felt rather insignificant when he saw his
one car of ore, upon which so much depended,
switched into the railroad yards beside the train

loads of ore from the large mines. A clerk took
the number of the car, the names of the owners,
and remarked very casually, "Your ore will go
through the crushers tomorrow morning at eight
o'clock. You will be allowed to watch the sample
taken, if you want to."

Clearly this man was not in the least impressed
by what Roy thought was a most important trans-
action. But Roy did not neglect his business because of the offhand manner of the clerk. He was
grateful for the experience he had had in preparing samples for assay under Catron's watch-
ful eyes. He went without lunch next day in order
to follow every step of the crushing and sampling.

At last, he was given a small package containing the check sample, which he took at once to a
local assayer for the final test. The man said he
would have the returns the following morning.
Roy spent a night of anxious waiting and slept
but little. He was at the assay office at nine
o'clock and got his certificate.

The assayer was very friendly. "Are you going
to ship here regularly?" he asked.

"I hope so, if our ore pays. This is my first shipment."

"I'll be glad to attend to the sampling and assaying of your ore," the man suggested. "You may inquire at the bank as to my reliability."

Roy looked at the certificate and saw with discouraged amazement that the total value as estimated by the assayer was only fifty dollars per ton and the weight given by the smelter scales was twenty-two tons. He rubbed his eyes and walked slowly down to the smelter office to get his small check. Despite the warnings given by Kemper and Catron, Roy had built his hopes too high. Like most inexperienced miners, he had expected the ore to run in carload lots as high as the best samples he had taken.

No greater disappointment can come to a prospector than when he reads the cold truth from smelter returns and learns that the check he had hoped would be thousands, is only for hundreds. In Roy's case it was doubly depressing because of the reported richness of the float that had been found on the surface directly above where the shipment had been mined. The check

Roy got that morning was for only nine hundred dollars after freight and smelter charges had been deducted. Roy recalled with an added pang of remorse that the royalty and expenses must be paid out of that. The net amount received for the carload would not repay what had been drawn from the bank.

On his return to the mine, Roy found that Frank had not counted so much on the returns as he had, and stood the shock better.

"I don't think it's too bad," Frank said. "Kemper says that if we can keep the trail open all winter and increase the production by putting on two shifts of miners, we can make the mine pay. At any rate, we would have work for the burros all winter instead of having them idle eight months out of the twelve."

The first night after Roy's return, the boys had a long conference with Kemper, who recommended that the boys keep on for at least six months, in spite of their discouraging start. He made an estimate on the amount an ore house, bunkhouse for six more men, and a stable for the stock would cost. He said that one thousand dollars would cover the expense of the buildings.

He suggested that the work might be speeded up by buying a pair of horses or mules to drag the logs from the timber to the place where they would be used. He knew that he could get a pair of good mules for two hundred and fifty dollars; this would include harness, chains and blankets for protection during the storms.

As a result of the talk, Roy decided to draw the remaining balance from the Del Norte bank and deposit it with the check from the smelter in a bank at Lake City. When this had been done, he went to the store with the smelter returns and gave Fields a check for the royalty. At Robinson's suggestion, Roy entered the amount of royalty paid on the back of the bond and lease, and asked Fields to sign his name below it.

The storekeeper's eyes shone greedily when he saw the first check he had ever received from the Iron Mask. "If you boys are going to work all winter, you better open an account for six months' supply. I'll carry you for any reasonable amount."

It was a comfort to Roy to know that a man as cautious as Fields was known to be should offer them credit, but he and Frank had decided that they would not go in debt if they could possibly avoid it.

"Thanks for the offer," Roy replied, "but we are going to make the mine pay its way, or we quit."

There was no question about the storekeeper's approval of this reply. "If we had more operators like you, the mining business would not have the bad name it now has," Fields remarked emphatically.

"We are going to put in supplies for a small crew," Roy told him. "I've heard of a cook that Mr. Robinson says is good. If I can get him, I'll have him place the order for a winter's supplies with you, to be filled as convenient. There'll be no great hurry about it, because we're going to keep the trail open and can pack supplies up at any time."

"I've always thought that trail could be kept open," Fields encouraged. "There may be days when you can't get over it, but if you wait until the snow settles and then break out the trail with a mule dragging a go-devil, the wind will build the snow up on the track and make good footing for your burros."

That evening Roy met Joe Bush, the man that Robinson had recommended as a cook. Roy was pleased with the cook's appearance and gave him a job for the winter.

"You better make out an order for enough supplies to last ten men six months. Get the best of everything. I know that the way to get good work out of men and keep them on the job is to feed them well."

"You're right about that," Bush answered. "While I may buy some things that you'll think are extravagant, in the end you'll find I've saved you money."

The following day Roy and the new cook rode up to the foot of the trail on the wagons that hauled the supplies. Frank and Kemper were waiting with the pack train and loaded the provisions at once and packed them to the Iron Mask.

Kemper fully approved of the decision the boys had made to work the mine all winter. "I'll pick up a man whenever I find a good one. We'll use him to help build the houses and promise him a job in the mine later. Most of these men are fair carpenters. When we get everything fixed for the winter, we'll really put out the ore. We can keep the burros busy all winter."

The miners had been working energetically during the days that had elapsed and had nearly another carload ready to sack. The vein had proved to be about six feet wide, half of which Kemper judged would be too low grade to ship. One thing puzzled the old miner. "I can't figure out what has become of the little seam we followed all the way through the trachyte," he told the boys. "There are several things we haven't found out about this vein. The deposit of mineral left in the small seam was richer than anything we've found here in the porphyry. That was what encouraged me to expect high grade ore here where the cross dyke held back the deposit from above."

"Maybe we should cross cut into the trachyte," Roy suggested.

Kemper took a pick and struck the wall a heavy blow, breaking the point of the pick. "I tried this before," he said. "You can see that the rock is too tight here to carry values. The only answer I get is that we may find richer ore towards the surface. As soon as we get our force organized, I'm going to start an up-raise."

"Then you've not given up hope of finding the rich ore?" Frank asked.

"Not quite. Some place on the east side of the trachyte there's a streak of high grade. I've seen float from up above here that would run a thousand dollars a ton. It's a cinch no one carried it there. Robinson thinks the same as I do," Kemper went on. "That little seam that led us through the trachyte brought values from a deposit somewhere above us, and that's what we're going to find or die trying."

Work began at once on the buildings. Roy went to the Lone Star and began packing up the assay outfit, carefully taking down the furnace so as not to injure the firebrick and tiling. Among his other treasures Roy found a number of expensive books on assaying, geology, mining and ore occurrence, which pleased him greatly.

Frank had made the acquaintance of a packer by the name of Zeke Anderson, who seemed to be steady and energetic. He hired him, and the two continued packing from the Legal Tender, relieving Kemper for more important work.

By the time Kemper had the building for the assay office completed, Roy had brought his equipment down, and the furnace was put up at once. It was a happy day for Roy when he ran the first samples in his own laboratory, and he was encouraged when he found that the samples he took from the vein for his test were the best he had assayed. These samples came from a small streak near the trachyte and showed small specks of mineral that Roy at first thought to be mere crystals. When he weighed the buttons and found that they indicated values of several hundred dollars a ton, he examined the uncrushed samples more closely under his new powerful microscope.

Roy thought it was barely possible that he might have found the source of the rich deposit that had been in the seam. Instead of telling Kemper what he hoped, he kept it to himself.

"I'm going to let Kemper work according to his own practical methods," Roy thought. "There's not much yet to support the idea I have as to the source of the rich ore, and I don't want to lead him away from his own plans."

The book on assaying that Roy had found with the assay outfit was a valuable acquisition. The instructions given in it were easy to understand. He had plenty of the reagents necessary for experimentation in the bottles on the shelves. His year of chemistry enabled him to read symbols and he was deeply interested in the experiments he made. After he had carefully checked a determination he had made for copper, he took some of the same pulp to Catron and asked him to run it. The result was encouraging, as Catron's returns were within one-tenth of one percent of his own.

Roy now got a big thrill out of being able to assay any of the ore that Kemper was in doubt about and as a result they discarded all the low grade material. Because of Roy's newly acquired skill, the next car shipped brought a considerable increase in the returns. After all deductions, the smelter check was for sixteen hundred dollars, which showed a good profit above all expenses, including even the building and the purchase of the assay outfit.

Kemper was jubilant. "I'll have the new houses finished by the first of November and, when we get all the men into the mine, we'll increase production to a car a week."

The boys were pleased when John and Andrew decided to stay at the mine for the winter.

"That's because of the grub that Bush is giving them," Kemper said. "We'll soon build up a boarding house reputation that will bring us the top crew of the whole country. Good grub, a comfortable place to work and warm cabins will attract miners better than high wages."

As the Legal Tender was more than a thousand feet higher than the Iron Mask, Woodruff did not think it wise to try to keep the trail to his property open after the first heavy snow came. He told Roy that if they succeeded in keeping the trail to the Iron Mask open, he might see if he could do the same with his trail another year.

"You fellows have sure got what it takes to get along in this country," Woodruff went on. "And if a blizzard should strike, I'll turn out my crew and help you open the trail."

Chapter 10

THE PROMISE TO HAVE the buildings completed by the first of November was kept, and Frank promptly filled the hay sheds with feed for the stock. Bush was directed to order whatever supplies he wanted for a Thanksgiving dinner, which pleased him.

"I'll throw a feed for them that will make this place the talk of the whole country," Bush said. "I know a rancher down on the Lake Fork that's feeding corn to a flock of turkeys and I'll write

182

him to save us birds enough for Thanksgiving and Christmas."

Now that the two crews were working in the tunnel, Roy found it difficult to prospect the sides of the vein next to the trachyte without getting in the way of the miners. He had gone into the mine once after the night shift had come off, but Kemper heard him and cautioned him against going back after the men had shot, as there might be loose rocks hanging above.

Among Roy's books was a very practical treatise on vein displacements and faulting. In it he had found an example similar to the one that had puzzled Kemper. It was something in this article that started Roy investigating the wall on the trachyte side of the vein. He now wanted to cross-cut the trachyte dyke.

Thanksgiving morning dawned bright and calm. Kemper had given the crew a day's layoff and all had gone to the Legal Tender to visit with the miners there. Kemper wanted to see Cadle about something and he too was away. It was the first day that the boys had been alone at the mine for some time. Roy was quick to seize the opportunity to make the experiment he had been thinking about for weeks.

No sooner were the men out of sight than he called Frank to come. He brought a set of sharp steel, a hammer and scraper from the blacksmith shop, and the two went in to the point in the tunnel where the seam they had followed had disappeared. About a foot from the place where the first low grade ore had been found, Roy measured off a distance of three feet and made a mark on the wall.

"Now what are you going to do?" Frank asked.

"You and I are going to drill a hole in this wall."

"What, into that trachyte? Are you crazy? It's harder than flint."

"All the same, we are drilling it," Roy said. "Do you want to hold or do the striking?"

Frank picked up a starter and spotted a hole just above the mark Roy had made. "O.K. I'll hold the drill. Let's see if you've forgotten how to hit."

Roy swung the hammer lightly until the bit of the drill began to cut through the outer surface, then he increased the force until he struck with all the power and skill he had. When Roy had been striking for half an hour, Frank took the hammer and did a turn. In this way they had drilled a hole about three feet deep, when Roy who was now striking felt the drill give under the hammer. He reduced the power of his next blow and looked inquiringly at his partner. Frank stuck out one finger as a signal for him to stop striking.

Roy's eyes shone expectantly. "What's happened?"

"Darned if I know, Roy. It seems as if the trachyte has turned soft."

"Let me take the drill a minute," Roy proposed. "Now strike very lightly."

In this manner they drilled a foot or more in a few minutes. Roy cleaned out the hole, saving every particle of the mud he took out. This mud was black as ink.

"Let's assay this," Roy proposed. "It looks good —but maybe I'm wrong." He hurried out to the assay office and put the scrapings in a small pan which he placed in the drier, while Frank hurriedly started a fire in the furnace.

While the muffle was heating, Roy explained

to Frank why he had made the experiment. He showed him a geological map he had made, showing the formation of the mountain from the old workings down to the point where they had drilled the hole.

"According to Professor Lake, there are frequently two parallel veins; or perhaps one vein with what geologists call 'a horse' of country rock between them. We've all been puzzled by the disappearance of the seam. I found several cross seams that I thought cut into the trachyte, but I wasn't sure. I've assayed the content of these seams and every one of them carries high silver values."

"You mean that the vein we've been working may not be the real one?"

"I didn't say that, Frank. In fact, it may be, from the angle of the formation we have drilled into, that it is the same vein, and that we were within a few inches of it where the seam disappeared in the wall. What we've been thinking was the wall is only 'a horse' of trachyte, not more than three feet in thickness. All the values we've found in the vein came from this streak we have just drilled into, which is in reality the hanging wall of the vein."

"Roy, you're a wonder!" Frank said admiringly. "I see now why you want to be a mining engineer. Whatever led you to think this through?"

"It was simple enough. The assays show that the values decrease the farther we get from the right-hand wall of the drift, which indicates that the source of enrichment lies in that direction. These books give example after example of the very thing we have been puzzling over."

"It's funny Kemper didn't think of it," Frank said.

"I'm surprised at that too, but it's understandable. Kemper's experience is all practical and limited to things he has seen. It happens that he has always found that the enrichment comes from above. You'll recall that he's been wanting to start an up-raise ever since we struck the vein."

"That's right. Say, Roy, the muffle is getting white hot."

"Good. Our sample is dry and I can run a scorifier test much quicker than a crucible assay."

Frank watched Roy weigh out one-tenth of an

assay ton of the dried mud. "What makes you take such a little bit?"

"Because, in assaying, everything is computed upon the basis of an assay ton. We only use one-tenth of an assay ton in scorification. That's the amount generally taken for a silver test. Later we'll run the ore for gold, then we'll use a half an assay ton and a twenty-gram crucible."

Bush had told the men that dinner would be ready at two o'clock, and shortly after noon they began to return to the mine. The boys were in the assay office when Kemper came in. "Hello, aren't you birds going to lay off even on a holiday?" he demanded.

"Kemper, look here," Roy called. "I think we've got something to show you."

Kemper looked over Roy's shoulder as he was taking the silver button out of the cupel. "Great ghost of Colorow, what's that from?"

"That is one-tenth of an assay ton of mud from a hole Frank and I drilled in the east wall about three feet from where we lost the little seam. We don't know how thick the ore is, but this sample will run about two thousand dollars a ton."

Roy explained his theory and the result of their

experiment, but before he got half way through, Kemper went to the powder box and got half a dozen sticks of dynamite. The boys went with him to load the hole they had drilled in the wall, which was quickly fired and exposed a vein of rich gray copper ore, that as nearly as Kemper could estimate was three feet wide. Kemper sampled the vein thoroughly, cutting one trench as far across the vein as it had been opened. "If that runs half as good as what you got out of the mud, you boys are rich."

"Let's not tell anyone until we get these check assays out. I don't want to be disappointed again," Roy said. "If this is the real thing, it will keep. By the time we've eaten Bush's big dinner the samples will be dry enough to crush and before we go to bed tonight we'll know the answer."

"Isn't it funny," Frank whispered, as they took their seats at the table, "that this should happen today."

Roy grinned happily. "We couldn't have picked a better day, could we?"

Bush had fulfilled his promise. The turkeys were cooked to a turn. He had everything that goes with such a feast and topped it off with a plum pudding that all pronounced The Best Ever.

The boys left the crew playing cards in the bunkhouse when they returned to the assay office. The samples confirmed Kemper's estimate. The one that had been taken clear across the vein ran eight hundred ounces in silver and ten ounces in gold.

"Think of it," Frank said wonderingly, "one ton of this ore is worth more than a whole carload of what we have been shipping."

"We might as well tell the men what's happened," Kemper said. "We have to square up the hole you shot in the vein and get the drift straightened out so that we can mine this bonanza."

"Then you're going to quit mining the other ore," Frank said.

"For the time, yes," Kemper replied. "You'll want to ship the rich ore until you have a comfortable bank account and your mine paid for. Next summer when the trails are dry, you can buy more burros and ship from both chutes."

The entire crew, including Bush and Zeke Anderson, the packer, went in to see the discovery. Kemper took a canvas bedcover off his own bed and laid it on the floor of the drift before he let anyone do any picking.

Old Andrew ran his big gnarled hands over the surface of the vein, "I think she been here all the time!" he said. Every one laughed.

Kemper tried to pry into the ground that had not yet been broken, but was unable to get any more of the mineral loose. He turned to the night shift. "When you fellows start work, put in four pop shots, load 'em light, not over a half a stick to a hole. We can't afford to waste any of this stuff."

One of the miners spoke to his partner. "We might as well work tonight."

"Sure. We can get this all squared up before morning and the day shift can start takin' out the money."

"You come out at twelve o'clock," Bush told them. "I've got the makin's of a lunch for the crowd."

The boys found sleep out of the question that night and put in the time until Bush called them to the midnight lunch, making changes in their plans. Kemper stayed in the mine in order to be sure that his instructions about the work were obeyed. At eleven o'clock, four muffled shots were heard and as soon as the smoke had cleared from the breast of the tunnel, the boys went back to see the result of the shots.

Kemper was again picking at the rock. "Those shots did the trick," he told them. "We've got the true wall this time. The rich ore is four feet wide and it looks like a true fissure vein."

The entire crew was treated to a midnight lunch of oyster stew, cold turkey and what remained of the plum pudding. All the talk ran to estimates on the value of the big strike. Some of the men who had worked in the mines around Silverton compared it to the Sunnyside and Gold King, both heavy producers.

Kemper was more conservative.

"She's big enough," he admitted. "If this chute holds for a hundred feet, which is likely, the Iron Mask is a bigger mine than the Legal Tender. The funny part is, that instead of its belonging to a stock company, with hundreds of stockholders, it belongs to two mighty fine kids who had what it takes to stick when the goin' got rough."

The night shift sacked twenty sacks of the high grade ore that night. Next day Kemper hired two experienced ore sorters to handle the ore in the ore house, throw out any waste that got in, and sew the sacks. The pile of sacks grew rapidly and the boys began to make plans.

"If this fine weather lasts for two weeks," Roy said, "we'll be able to ship at least one, perhaps two, cars and get the returns on them in time so that we can go out for Christmas."

"Whatever you say," Frank rejoined. "The burros are feeling fine since we began feeding them oats, and we're loading three hundred pounds to the jack and making two trips a day. I told the teamsters to begin hauling to the railroad tomorrow. I find that they've two empties ready to receive the shipment. A week more should turn the trick."

One morning Roy saw Kemper glance up at Carson Peak and shake his head. "This is too mild; it isn't seasonable. We'll have a storm inside of twenty-four hours, and when it comes we'll pay for these weather breeders we've been having." He sent men into the timber that day and put the mules to work snaking in a huge supply of mine timbers and firewood.

Toward evening Roy noticed filmy clouds hanging around the top of the peak, and remembered seeing the same conditions just before the heavy storm the winter before. He called Frank into the assay office. "If we're going to move the stock down to the old camp at the foot of the trail, we'd better get at it before a storm begins."

"Right you are, Partner. Zeke is packing the shoeing outfit and extra saddles now. We'll be ready to get out of here inside of an hour."

"Then, I think now is the time for me to tell you what I've been figuring that we should plan for the winter."

"O.K. Let's have it."

"We both realize that we owe our success largely to Kemper."

"No argument on that score," Frank said. "I've felt all along that if we actually did make a go of the mine, he's entitled to something more than just the wages he agreed to take."

"I'm with you. The thing resolves itself to this.

We either give him full charge of the mine so that we can go on with our plans for an education, or one of us will have to stay here to attend to the shipments and pay the bills."

Frank's face sobered. "I sure hate to give up the idea of going to school, but if you want me to, I'll stick."

"I don't think that's necessary. Suppose we let Kemper take charge of the work, keep the men's time, and attend to the shipments, using his own judgment as to the class and amount of ore to ship, and have complete charge of the whole business at a good salary?"

"It seems to me that would be the thing to do. But how about the assaying and the settlements with the smelter?"

"That can be arranged. The School of Mines at Golden is very generous with their students. The faculty encourages men to use the laboratory for experimentation. I'm sure that they will let me run whatever samples Kemper wants assayed. He can direct the smelter to send the controls to me. I will assay them and make settlement. From the samples we have taken of the vein, I know that the mine will not only pay well, but will give us enough profit so that we can go through school comfortably. We can spend our summer vacations here and, if Kemper needs anything, one of us can come back any time."

"Let's call Kemper in and see what he thinks of the idea," Frank suggested.

The old miner listened soberly as the boys outlined their plans. Tears came to his eyes as he realized the confidence they were willing to place in him. After a minute he got control of himself, and his face lighted up with the enthusiasm that had often helped them during the dark days.

"There's no reason why it can't be done," Kemper said. "We know that the shipments will pay all expenses and give you a nice balance each month. If the snow gets too deep for the stock, we'll lay off until the weather settles, then work double time to catch up. We'll ship nothing but the high grade ore during the winter. The low grade stuff we'll pile up until such a time as you build a mill to treat it here."

"We hadn't thought of that," Frank put in.

"I've figured that you'd do that sometime,"

Kemper went on. "I've done some panning on this low grade ore. It concentrates about four into one and the loss is not heavy." He turned to Roy: "Since you are going to the School of Mines you can get all the dope on modern ore dressing and determine just what machinery you'll need for this type of ore. During the winter you can have plans drawn for a mill. I'll guarantee that by the time the snow is off next summer, you'll have enough money in the bank to buy the machinery and start putting up the building."

The talk with Kemper gave the boys a new interest—something tangible to work toward during the winter, and to look forward to during the next summer vacation.

One of the men who had been working in the ore house was a good packer, and he was put on the train with Zeke so that Frank was free to go with Roy. The changes were quickly made and two days later the boys shook hands with their crew and rode their skis down the mountain to the new camp, where the burros that had served them so faithfully were comfortably quartered for the winter.

A week later Frank registered at the University

of Colorado and Roy was welcomed at the State School of Mines. Their goal for an education was reached and the future looked bright, thanks to the Iron Mask Mine and their own hard work.

Glossary

ASSAY TON   A standard weight by which is calculated the amount of gold or silver in a ton of the ore from which the small amount assayed has been taken as a "sample."

ASSAYER   A person skilled in the analysis of ore to determine the amount of one or more metals.

BALANCES   Delicate scales used for weighing. Those used in this operation are sensitive to one one-thousandth of a milligram and are very expensive.

BOND and LEASE	A legal document in which an owner grants the right of occupancy and development of a mining property to another, conveying the privilege of purchase.
BUCKBOARD	A highly polished plate of flat iron, usually three feet square, used for pulverizing ore.
BURN	A forest through which a fire has run, killing the timber but not destroying it. This is also called "fire-killed" timber.
CRUCIBLE	A small vessel made of fire clay or porcelain, used for melting ore.
CUPEL	A small, shallow, porous cup made of bone ash, used in assaying.
DRIFT	A tunnel along a vein is called a drift, and one at right angles to the vein or drift is a cross-cut.
DUTCH OVEN	A small cast iron bowl with a heavy iron cover, used for baking over a bed of charcoal.
DYKE (or Dike)	A wall or upthrust of rock cutting through older formations.
FAULTING	A slipping of rock beneath the surface of the ground.
FLOAT	Broken pieces of ore or quartz that indicate the presence of mineral.

FLUX   Any substance such as borax or lime
                    used to fuse metals. (See Fusing)

FULMINATING   Any highly explosive powder.
Powder

FURNACE   The furnace used in assaying is made
                   of brick, fire clay and tile, tightly
                   bound with angle iron. It is so ar-
                   ranged that the draft is from below and
                   creates an intensive heat around a
                   muffle or long, low oven made of fire-
                   brick.

FUSING   To liquefy by heat.

GO-DEVIL   Two logs usually ten feet in length
                   bolted together at one end, the other
                   end braced apart making a wedge.
                   Used in dragging heavy machinery
                   short distances and in breaking a road
                   through snow drifts.

HAND LEVEL   A small metal tube having a bubble
                   of air confined in glass, which remains
                   constant when the instrument is held
                   horizontal. An arc graduated to 180
                   degrees is fastened to the side and
                   enables one to calculate the slope or
                   "pitch" of the ground.

HARD ROCK   Men trained to drill holes for dy-
MINER   namite in hard rock such as trachyte
                   or granite.

IRON BED   A considerable tract of land containing bog iron or low grade oxide of iron.

LAGGING   In mining—a straight, smooth pole of varying length used to make a floor above the drift to support the vein-matter broken down in the process of mining.

MUFFLE   An oven used in a furnace to heat the contents without exposing them directly to the fire.

MULE SKINNER   A man who works with mules either as a driver or a packer.

PACK TRAIN   A number of burros or mules used for transporting freight, ore and timbers over a trail inaccessible to trucks or wagons. Thirty or more loose burros constitute a train. Fifteen mules handled by one man is called a "string."

PATENTED LAND   Land to which the government has granted exclusive title to an individual is called "patented."

PORPHYRY   A rock of crystals embedded in a dark red or purple base.

POSTS and CAPS   Two posts, usually six feet long, are used to support a "cap" of four feet, which in turn supports the lagging.

POWDER
WARMER
    Dynamite, 40 percent Nitro, will not explode when frozen and miners use "double boilers" to thaw the sticks, heating the water in the outside can with candles. These are generally homemade appliances.

REAGENT
    Any chemical or material used in the treatment of ore to produce a proper fusion.

RIFFLE
    A set of small tin troughs with open spaces between them. Used in accurately reducing the volume of ore to be assayed.

SCORIFIER
    A small flat vessel of fire clay used in melting ore.

STULL
    A heavy piece of timber wedged between the walls of a vein to support lagging.

TIMBER HITCH
    The manner in which the rope attached to the saddle is tied. There are a number of different hitches which can be better illustrated than described.

TIMBERJACK
    A man skilled in the use of an axe is called a Timberjack to distinguish him from the men who work in the saw mills.

TRACHYTE
    A close-grained, very hard rock, generally carrying no mineral values.